Memoria

To my mother

Memoria

a novel

by Louise Dupré

Translated by Liedewy Hawke

SIMON & PIERRE

A MEMBER OF THE DUNDURN GROUP

TORONTO · OXFORD

Editors: Barry Jowett, Marc Côté, Shirley Knight Morris
Printer: Transcontinental Printing Inc.

Canadian Cataloguing in Publication Data
Dupré, Louise, 1949–
[Memoria. English]
Memoria
Translation of: La memoria
ISBN 0-88924-287-9

I. Hawke, Liedewy. II. Title. III. Title: Memoria. English.
PS8557.U66M3513 1999   C843'.54   C99-930509-3
PQ3919.2.D849M44 1999

1   2   3   4   5   03   02   01   00   99

THE CANADA COUNCIL | LE CONSEIL DES ARTS
FOR THE ARTS | DU CANADA
SINCE 1957 | DEPUIS 1957

We acknowledge the support of the **Canada Council for the Arts** for our publishing program. We also acknowledge the support of the **Ontario Arts Council** and the **Book Publishing Industry Development Program** of the Department of **Canadian Heritage**.

Care has been taken to trace the ownership of copyright material used in this book. The author and the publisher welcome any information enabling them to rectify any references or credit in subsequent editions.

Printed and bound in Canada.

Printed on recycled paper.

Set in Weiss
Designed by Scott Reid

Simon & Pierre
8 Market Street
Suite 200
Toronto, Canada
M5E 1M6

Simon & Pierre
73 Lime Walk
Headington, Oxford,
England
OX3 7AD

Simon & Pierre
2250 Military Road
Tonawanda NY
U.S.A. 14150

Stroll by our house once in a while,
Give a thought to the days when we were all still together,
But don't linger too long.

Mario Luzi

First Song

The Little Girl Who Loved Birds

Chapter One

Days never start off the same way, it all depends on how we open our eyes. Often our eyelids are so heavy they almost won't come unstuck. And we lie there ensnared by the night, the nebulous, pitch-black night where no smells of earth or incense reach us, motionless, until in spite of ourselves a finger moves and, after that, a hand. Then the day takes us by surprise and we return to the light. We say, "I'm alive" to position ourselves in the middle of things. Yes, this woman turning her eyes toward the window is really me. In a few moments I'll make myself sit up, I'll place my feet on the varnished wood. Once again I'll be up. As if there were nothing unusual about that.

10   But sometimes the morning softly enfolds us, the sky
already a perfect curve, our head full of music, of wide-open
spaces, and we quickly get up. In the flower bed peonies are
beginning to open, summer has entrenched itself a little
more. We chase away a mynah bird who is quarrelling with a
robin. We can't imagine there being any other danger. For a
few minutes we are eight years old.

I used to put my head underneath the pillow when I
heard Mama push the door open. Like an ostrich, I played at
burying my head in the sand. I could almost feel the warm
grains against my cheeks, my lips, the outer edges of my
ears. "Come on, girls, seven o'clock, time to get ready."
Always the same phrase, the same intonation, the same
slightly mechanical cheeriness. In her bed right beside me,
my little sister Noëlle was giggling. Philippe had come in, he
was tickling her with his jam-covered hands. He was trying
to climb into her bed, but Mama gathered him in her arms
and carried him back to the kitchen to clean him up.

I would make up a story while slipping on my blue-and-
white uniform. Have I already told you?

This morning the day begins where yesterday left off. In
total chaos. I had been hoping for a miracle, I think. The
books, the boxes of dishes, the clothes, the bedding would
all have been in place when I woke up. I would have had
time to read. Or perhaps continue with my translation? We
never know first thing in the morning if the words are going
to form coherently on the square-patterned sheet of paper.

I haven't been able to finish my book. Since you left I
have been accumulating great masses of notes. Some
images come to me, but they can't find their proper place
in the sentences, they all huddle together, they hiccup.
How could I explain this to you, though, since you fight
every day against the forces that act upon materials? But I
have an excuse. I am fixing up my new place. Should the
walls between the kitchen and the dining-room be
knocked down? Or the bathroom enlarged? It's too small.
They always are in structures built in the thirties. Yes, I do
have an excuse.

Surprises come along, too — days that pull us away into unexpected worlds. A phone call, a visit from a friend. A contract. We ask if we can have a couple of hours to think it over, and we accept. Can one afford to say no when one is a freelancer? The next time the job will be offered to someone else.

Some days the wheel stops on a lucky number. Bright golden sunshine, the flaky pastry of a croissant, a foreign poet we've discovered in a bookstore, a song that moves us, and suddenly the words offer themselves up, the light draws us in. That reality delights me, the one that glides through the shadows.

When I was eleven, I dreamt of a life of ecstasy, in the evening, in May, as I walked home from church, hymns and incense still lingering in my head. Alone. Without Noëlle. Without Philippe or François — little François who was *not* expected, Mama would whisper into the telephone. "We found him in the cabbage patch," she had answered when Noëlle questioned her. "Wabbit patch, wabbit patch," Philippe chanted, waving his pink toy rabbit. Mama had smiled but not said another word. The mystery remained unsolved. And yet I knew there was some truth to her answer. Her stomach had swollen up until it became a round greenhouse and one night François had burst out of it, like a bush from a confined space. Mother as nourishment, mother as a garden.

I wasn't going to have any children. No baths to give, no sniffles or scraped knees to take care of, no meals to cook. When I was grown up I would live a life filled with passion, like heroines in novels. One's whole existence contained in the verb "to love," active voice, passive voice, past, present, future, future anterior, future perfect. On my deathbed, I would ask for the word "love" to be inscribed on my eyelids.

Chapter Two

I'm trying to understand.

Perhaps I might easily have become that nurse dressed in white who is slowly walking along, already tired of the heat of the day which has only just started. Or that woman trotting past the house, trying to keep up with her child. In any life another life may suddenly emerge without warning, and the first one goes out of kilter, it wages war against us until we're utterly exhausted. By the time we've recovered a bit we no longer recognize ourselves. That's what happened to you — you were unable to defend yourself.

I am waiting. Every morning I wait. Impossible to begin anything until the postman has been. A quick cup of coffee and I sit down at my desk by the window. Now and then I get distracted. The room looks very pretty. The wall behind the bookcases a delicate shade of orange, I'm happy with the effect, the flower-patterned armchair bought on sale, and that walnut coffee table where I've put the blue vase you brought back for me from Singapore. Only one month, yet I missed you so much it made my head swim. But you returned, you were still in love with me, and the bedroom lit up again. We would always be together is what you said, and I believed you.

No news from you. Nothing, for six months now. You might have got lost in an endless jungle, have fallen into the hands of a terrorist group, you might be dead. Or have found a new happiness. One moment I see you with an explorer's helmet, and in the next, blindfolded in a dungeon crawling with vermin, or sometimes with your hair streaming behind you, eyes shining.

There will have to be a letter from you in the mailbox one morning, I stubbornly keep telling myself. One cannot erase ten years just like that, life isn't a magic notepad.

For Noëlle I used to draw large houses, you know, with windows, then when I lifted up the plastic-coated sheet everything disappeared. But I had pressed hard on the pencil and the house remained imprinted on the slate underneath. It was superimposed on the trees, the birds, the cats, the rope-skipping little girls and the mothers who watched them. It formed a strange landscape, yet I was able to make it out. None of the pictures were erased.

I would imagine you still feel some emotion when you happen to remember for a moment how my voice grows hoarse when I start to laugh. I imagine you do. Now I notice a sort of quiver in my voice when I don't pay attention. But you will probably never hear it.

3
Chapter Three

Inside our chest there is a muscle where our hurts are stored up — the slap from Papa when we were four years old and had broken a china ornament, the undeserved punishment we received at school, our defeats, our disappointments in friendship and love. Yes, disappointments in love. All that together becomes a lump, a tight lump which, as time passes, weighs more and more heavily on our heart and makes it difficult to breathe. People may say this is the common lot of humanity in all its weakness — but it's no use, no one can comfort us. Every sorrow is the only one in the world.

I hadn't seen anything coming. Perhaps some slight signs of fatigue when you came back to the apartment after work. You would absent-mindedly kiss me and shut yourself up in your study. "So much work," you'd say by way of apology.

Sometimes I asked if I could come and join you, I wouldn't disturb you. I just wanted to sit close to your table, feel close to you, your furrowed brow, the smell of your cigarette, and that way you had of scratching yourself behind your left ear with a pencil when you were searching for a solution to a problem. You were making small changes to the plan of a museum, costs had to be taken into consideration.

"Reality is such a bore!" Your gravelly voice. The untidy room. The fern was hidden behind stacks of scientific journals. You were constantly rummaging around looking for your papers, but you always managed to find them — in a bookcase, underneath a filled ashtray or on the threadbare Persian carpet left over from your student days. On the notice-board, photos from our last vacation reflected our love. My mind was at ease.

I didn't see anything coming. Your voice on the phone was neutral that afternoon, at least I think it was. You suggested I meet you at a restaurant, I didn't sense the trap. An evening with you, how long had it been? I slipped on my black dress, your favourite, and decided to leave right away. I wouldn't be able to copy out another sentence. Even November was lovely in the drizzle. I would walk to the subway.

On the platform a shabbily dressed man paced up and down waving his arms about. "This day is doomed," he shouted, but the crowd around him hurried along ignoring him. I felt a pang of sadness, I would never get used to distress. Then the train came. I stepped into the car and forgot.

Emotions, sensations, images all surge back and forth like a stormy tide and I am almost swept away. So I sometimes forget. It's only bit by bit that I've managed to re-establish the chain of events. Your arrival, the dry martini you had as an aperitif, the nervous swinging of your left leg when you began to talk to me. Nothing was

16   going well any more, you needed a change. You had just accepted that contract in Brazil. I must have asked some naïve question, when you were planning to come back, for example. How could I really understand? You mumbled, "I don't think I'll be back."

The tables started to revolve around us, my head began to spin. I couldn't possibly get up. I stayed glued to that chair, yet I needed to run away, run away as fast as I could from that place cluttered with fake plants and Italian actresses, Lollobrigida, Sophia Loren, and others too imitating them in bold poses. Just then the waiter arrived to take our order. I said to him, "Help me, I'm going to faint."

Suit, tie, sweater, leather jacket, I can't remember what you were wearing that evening. I simply can't. I stumbled out without taking my coat, I hailed a taxi, I mechanically gave our address. I had only one thought — to curl up in bed under the covers.

You didn't follow me. You stayed there among the Italian actresses. You had already left me.

Chapter Four

The sky is too blue today, so perfect it overwhelms me, and that carries me back to my fragile state, my slightly hunched shoulders, the shadows under my eyes.

"Clouds hidden, Emma?" Noëlle would ask in that worried voice of hers, abandoning her spade in the sandbox for a moment. Where were the clouds hidden? Each time I gave her an older-sister kind of answer. Behind the sun, under the trees, in the garden. Then she could finish what she was building.

Noëlle, so afraid of everything — the wind, the dark, ghosts — nobody knew why. Did we really look like two sisters born twenty-three months apart? She, brown-haired

18   and rosy, eyes so pale they almost seemed unreal, that
melancholy smile. A premature child who hadn't been able
to hold on to the walls of the womb. *I* was dark, sturdy for
my age. I thought life was going to be a string of delights,
castles with drawbridges protecting us at the right time.
Even danger wouldn't be scary. It would be clear-cut, easy to
foresee, the dragon one slays with a single arrow.

Mama knew about Noëlle. I didn't. I hadn't learned to
predict the future yet. I took that up after the tragedy — I
mean after my sister disappeared. So I might try to read in
the tarot the things no one could understand.

Just before the Christmas break Bénédicte had come to
school carrying a small parcel done up with red ribbon.
Faithful friend that she was, she had sat down at our table in
the cafeteria as she did every other morning. She put the
present down in front of me. With trembling hands I
carefully removed the paper which was covered with tiny
bells and holly. I opened the cardboard box, spread out all
the cards on the Formica tabletop but couldn't figure out
what they meant. Bénédicte couldn't either. Inside the box,
though, we discovered a sheet with explanations.

The bell rang but we didn't hear it. The holidays had
started, now at least they wouldn't be total hell: Mama's
swollen eyes, Papa's stubborn silence, Philippe and François
getting into trouble, anxious for a bit of attention. The next
day I had hunted up a guide to the interpretation of the tarot
at the municipal library. I was going to have two weeks all to
myself. When I returned to school in January, I would know
how to read cards.

"Get our your tarot cards." Bénédicte just phoned me.
She is back, happy with the news reports she did in South
America. She is coming over this afternoon. I will lay the
face cards out on the table as I've done so many times — the
Star, the World, Temperance — all those great triumphs I
predicted for her. How many have come true? That doesn't
matter. Each time we meet she consults me, it's the tie that
has always bound the two of us together.

I have lost the gift of clairvoyance. I don't know if I will tell her. Now I can only see where things should go in the house. I am putting everything away, winter coats in the hall closet, bone china in the dresser, your belongings, all your belongings, in a closed room upstairs. Sometimes I push the door slightly open and look in: your swivel chair, your desk covered with boxes of books, the lingering smell of tobacco smoke — then you begin to exist again.

I haven't just imagined this love. It wasn't a dream, I don't think. But I cannot be completely sure, even when I look at our photographs. A part of my reality has split off from me, it's drifting in space, out of reach, and I'm desperately trying to catch hold of it again. I'm filled with fear. That's what I have left. Fear. The wind. I cling to the ground so as not to be blown away. I've become just like Noëlle. An empty shell.

Chapter Five

"To me you are still the little girl who loved birds." You adored the house, its wooden panelling, creaky floors, oak staircase and also the red maple in front, the squirrels, and the swallow whose nest is hidden away in the ivy on the balcony. The little girl who loved birds, you hugged me while you said this. As I opened my eyes, I smiled. I reached out for the alarm, ten o'clock — was I sleeping well again?

"Remission." The word came into my mind when I was making coffee. I repeated it several times, articulating each syllable, and went upstairs to get the dictionary. A temporary lessening, abatement of the disease. A respite, a period of quiet, a break. A rest.

What caught my attention was "temporary." The pain would come back. But I didn't care. Around me was a radiant silence and, dancing through the silence, clusters of light. I smiled again.

I'm looking better, Bénédicte pointed out as soon as she got here. I wanted to tell her about my dream, but not right away. First show her through my new refuge. Lifting up her arms, she let out whoops of delight at everything — a real buy, this house, how had I found it? Well, through an ad in the paper! An elderly woman, Madame Girard, wanted to sell quickly. Her husband had just died and her son was worried — too many rooms to look after for someone living alone. Too many memories as well. She cried in the lawyer's office. I would take very good care of her house, I solemnly promised her.

I hadn't told anyone about this incident, hadn't even thought of doing so. I now told Bénédicte. "You are wallowing in your loneliness," is how she answered. She throws daggers at someone's face without worrying she might hurt them. Words don't wound her, they form little bubbles around her that disappear into the air straightaway. She doesn't realize how harsh those words can be when she flings them at someone in that peremptory tone. Sadness darkened the wall, but Bénédicte immediately said something about her tactlessness and the wall became white again, smooth and white. That's a natural ability of hers — without apologizing, she gets people to forgive her. They forgive her because she's so generous. At school she had been the one who had found the right words. I will never forget how she acted after Noëlle disappeared.

Today, this souvenir from Ecuador, a gorgeous round tablecloth the colour of unbleached linen, a present that would bring me luck, she explained, as I gushed over it. The saleswoman, a shopkeeper with wrinkled hands, had promised her that. And the music filling the dining-room: a souvenir from a previous trip.

I spread the cards out on the table. She asked me a dozen questions all at the same time and I came up with

22   answers full of hope, of new plans, of love affairs. She
laughed, shared her secrets with me, asked me if we should
go and stir the sauce. Through the kitchen wafted delicious
smells of thyme and basil. I had cooked a meal, soup, a main
dish, dessert. The house was lived in. Once again. It was re-
entering the cycle of the seasons.

Chapter Six

Through the kitchen window, if I crane my neck a little, I can see a patch of dark grey tinged with pink. The lights of the city flow into it as into a lake and cover up the stars. It's not the whole heaven, barely a little square, but a sky nevertheless. It makes me look up for a moment.

Ten o'clock. Soon the woman next door will rest her huge bosom on the balcony railing, then I'll hear her warm velvety voice. And I will let myself be lulled by it. Every evening at ten, the same lament in Spanish. Sadness travels through every language.

There isn't a sound until nightfall, her curtains stay closed. Then, at dusk, the house comes to life. I can see the

24 woman coming out, her salt-and-pepper hair pulled back into a chignon. On her clothesline she hangs out gigantic flowered dresses made from cheap cotton. And men's trousers, check shirts. That must be the husband, but I've yet to see him. Then she goes down the steps with a scraping-tool in her hand and heads for the garden. Her thick fingers dig into the soil. She pulls out the weeds, replaces the earth. She tidies up her flowers — roses, pansies, gardenias — talking to them all the while in words with onomatopoeic sounds.

I listen to her every evening. As though her lament could heal me. But that's only a dream. Each life, I know, turns around on itself, spinning faster and faster, until one night it fades away forever. It's the end of the world each night for someone, but it isn't really the end. The city is still the city, beautiful and barbarous, the sprawling skyline, the dull roar. People go on breathing. Presence and absence meet in one and the same breath.

Sometimes I tremble, and I go out — I walk, I need to walk. Or run. When we had quarrelled, Noëlle and I, we would start running, we'd run until we were exhausted. Then we'd collapse on the grass and lie there totally still until our heartbeats slowed down, while we searched for sheep and woolly dogs, up there, in the immensity above us.

We would take each other's hand. Behind us, in some forgotten corner of our childhood, strewn among white pebbles and shabby fluffy toys, we have left dozens of reconciliations. We wouldn't know until much later that one life is connected to another only by the thinnest of threads.

7

Chapter Seven

I really wanted to take you to the airport. To see you put your luggage on the conveyor belt, to wait with you until they assigned you a seat in the smoking section by a window. The airline employee would have asked me if I was boarding too. I would have simply shaken my head and not cried. We would have had one last drink while watching the maintenance people bustling about on the runway. I would have followed you right up to the gate and stayed until the very last moment that I could possibly see you.

You refused. You didn't want me there as you brought our life together to a close. In your mind I had joined those other women you had loved — Dominique, your first real

26   love, and Judith, your first wife. You had already relegated me to a quiet, remote spot in your memory.

That offhand way you had when you talked to me about Judith. It was *my* fur, *my* fur alone you wanted to feel, dark, thick, soft, underneath your fingers. Now I occasionally picture other, even darker fur.

I have no interest in seduction any more. Like Mama, after François. She had stopped wearing make-up, no longer wore light rather low-cut dresses which revealed her rounded breasts as she bent over. She never went back to her old size. Did Papa still find her attractive, I wonder? At least he tried to reassure her, "A full-figured woman is beautiful." She pretended to believe him, helped herself to a second piece of cake, another cup of tea, then she read the paper and commented on the news, all the while keeping an eye on François in his honey-coloured wooden playpen.

I liked dessert time — the pictures in the newspaper, the soldiers with their helmets, the politicians accompanied by lovely women in evening gowns. Our slightly faded kitchen, the old wood-burning stove, Mama's apron and, behind her bulging bosom, her sleeping heart.

At the market, Monsieur Quintal no longer courted Mama. He sounded so neutral now when he asked her if she would like anything else. I needn't worry any more. Before, he used to murmur as he weighed a piece of meat, "You look gorgeous today." He emphasized each word and Mama blushed. An indefinable gleam would appear in her eye, as when Papa put his arm around her some evenings and leaned over to kiss her. A bell jar suddenly covered her. It was no use tugging at her sleeve because she wouldn't respond. Mama wasn't our mother any more, she even had her first name back. I heard, "Aline," uttered in a funny, throaty voice, and I was concerned.

I lifted Philippe out of his stroller, put him down on the floor. Squeals of delight. He started to run and Noëlle and I, laughing, caught him under the stalls. Around us, the shopkeepers were becoming impatient. Only then Mama remembered — three children, and the oldest wasn't any more sensible than the younger ones. She would tell us off, quickly pay Monsieur Quintal and take us to the produce section. I had won.

Bénédicte calls her mother by her first name. I couldn't do that. It's not a question of respect, it isn't. It just seems to me Aline doesn't suit her. That name looks toward the future, it is exactly right for the cheeky girl who is smiling in the photographs, staring straight into the eye of the camera.

In the photos of Mama, Monsieur Quintal isn't there. He lives in other pictures with another woman and other children. No matter how long I searched, all I could find was the family. Here, a wedding portrait. There, Mama and me. Then Papa holding the two of us, the girls. And later, Philippe as well as François joining the group and Mama, her body's fire now extinguished, contented no doubt, enjoying that simple kind of happiness that follows renunciation.

I will not give up. I will buy my almond cream and lovely sheer stockings that wrap my thighs in glossy lace. I will walk into the house one day with my legs and skin that used to light up your eyes. You'll be sitting on the sofa waiting for me. You'll kiss me, my face, my neck, my breasts, as you dig your nails a little bit into my back. I will know then that you have returned.

Chapter Eight

It's here. A beautiful street, wide and green, facing the park. Sturdy dogs being walked after work. Oak doors with leaded-glass windows. On the east side, my friend Bénédicte's apartment, but it has lost some of its character now that it has been renovated.

I must make the effort to ring. She will come and open the door, she'll kiss me. I'll go into the living-room where her colleagues are — press, radio, television — I've already met several of them at parties at her place. I'll smile and talk and I will lie.

I am that stranger pressing the bell, elegant in her ankle-length silk dress and short, neat, curly hair. Nobody will be able to guess about the tight lump weighing down on my heart. But in a couple of hours I will have my real face back, swollen because of the tears that keep welling up. For now I will just slip quietly into a space beside the humming universe.

I hardly have time to step inside. Someone picks me up, whirls me around. Vincent. It really is the same Vincent from fifteen years ago. "I'm back home," he says, "for good." He is joking. At forty-eight one should know what one wants.

Bénédicte's dark eyes sparkle with excitement, she almost forgets her hostess role. She makes plans — movies, picnics, exhibitions — and why not that old rock group's concert next week for old times' sake? Yes, I'd like to. But Vincent notices a slight hesitation in my voice.

"In any case, we'll kidnap you." Vincent has always known how to disarm me, I simply have to laugh. All the muscles in my face relax. He puts his arm around my shoulders. "So tell me." He is waiting. I am not a good student, I botch up my homework, I rattle on about anything. The house, the translation which will have to be handed in soon. Yes, I'm still freelancing. No, I haven't taken a holiday this summer.

And then — how is it possible? it must be the rosé, the heat of the apartment, or the noise — I begin to tell him, almost indiscreetly I tell him, what happened last winter. First about last fall. I describe that fateful evening, my efforts to make you stay, the utterly dismal Christmas season, and the day you left. Then I sort out what has happened since you went away. I tell Vincent everything, even how ashamed I feel of not being loved any more, of not being worthy of love, of not being cherished enough to be tucked in at night before I go to sleep.

Vincent scoffs at this. "What a crazy idea!" I know. I am crazy and I know it. But some day, I hope, every gesture I make will be playful again. I'll fluff up my hair, toss my head, strike seductive poses. I'll have the poise of those women who have always decided for themselves how long their love affairs would last. Suddenly I know this.

30   "But you're free now." With a flourish he puts his arm around my waist, he laughs, we both laugh. The whole day is swept up in that laugh which rings out like a Sunday.

9

Chapter Nine

I am not coping.

I came right out and confessed this to Bénédicte. She answered, "At least you're admitting it. That's the first step to recovery." Then she summoned the waiter with a casual wave. He came over to our table, visibly impressed. Was she really the one who was on television? Such wonderful news reports! What was she working on at the moment? She pleasantly answered his questions, chatted with him — she loved to be recognized. I was alone all of a sudden in that fake English pub. I stared down at the menu, at the hundreds of names of exotic beers, but my gaze was really focused on that place where heartaches begin, the big

32   ones and the small ones, and those that were inevitably yet to come.

The waiter had left again. I was going to answer Bénédicte that it was no use buying a house and repainting every room, I was simply marking time, going around in circles, not getting anywhere. There came a point when one had to admit that. But surprise! Vincent was heading toward us, beaming. What a wonderful coincidence! He had marvellous news and was taking us out to dinner. I didn't suspect for a moment that this meeting might have been arranged behind my back.

I suggested an Indian restaurant where I'd never gone with you. The Eastern music, the bunches of dried flowers, red-and-white chequered tablecloths and colourful towns on the walls all gave it a Latin Quarter atmosphere I was sure we would enjoy. For a few hours we would revisit a past embroidered with flowers, peace and old love affairs.

Vincent started off the reminiscing. He kissed Bénédicte's hand to show her he hadn't forgotten. Three wonderful years together, wild desire, promises. Then their love had worn thin, the way sheets do — people wake up one morning absolutely amazed they've slept for so long in the same bed. A break-up without scenes, Bénédicte had agreed. They'd managed to remain friends.

And what about Martin? It had been a long time since I'd seen my first lover. Recently I'd spotted an article by him in a history journal. Even though it was written in scholarly language, I had read it in one sitting, searching for something that was typical of him, some word or expression that would remind me of a gesture he used to make, his hand drawing spirals in the air as he spoke, or his teeth nibbling at my earlobes. But nothing had come back to me, I had felt no emotion, I would never have believed that we had spent five years together. A strange shadow under the lamp, something like a long scar. I had closed the journal, shelved it in the pine bookcase, the one he'd given me for my twenty-first birthday. The one where I put the books I wasn't going to keep.

Vincent filled our glasses. It was getting noisier, we were having to strain our voices. I turned around. Beside us, two blond girls had opened out a map and were talking in a guttural language. I had a sudden vision of Noëlle. Perhaps it was the paleness of the blonder one, a kind of resignation that could have been taken for otherworldliness. Bénédicte noticed too. For a moment we were separated from Vincent, connected as we were to each other by a shared knowledge of the world, that tragic sort of knowledge that covers our eyes like a veil. I thought, we grope about in the dark without being able to make sense of things. We would like to run away but we don't.

"Still no news?" Vincent reminded us he was there. He hadn't known Noëlle but had heard her story at least a hundred times. One night in November she had vanished like a ghost into the mist, and since then, nothing. For over twenty years now, absolutely nothing. There had been no solution to this infinity of nothing — perhaps Noëlle had never existed. I must have raised my voice. When I stopped talking, the two blond girls were watching me with a worried look. I forced a smile. Shyly they went back to their map.

There are people for whom the word "end" has a meaning, because they can trace back the chain of events. Sad people, but their minds are at rest. The small circle of new beginnings is outlined on the horizon. I had a sudden vision of Noëlle's face. Maybe it took inconsolable grief to get through other grief.

10

Chapter Ten

It is raining hard. An infinite number of tiny needles shatter against the windowpane with a crackling autumn sound and dripping-wet leaves dance among the words on my desk. I cannot concentrate. Yet this translation has to be handed in in a month.

That familiar lump is there again, in my chest — it takes up all the space between my ribs. But it isn't gripping me as tightly. Now there are times when I manage to calm it down, I can breathe freely then.

It isn't sadness. No. A fear rather, imminent danger that could destroy everything. The house, the text in front of me, my body, the whole planet. I don't stir, whatever I do I mustn't move. Or resist. All I can do is wait until bit by bit the world becomes a peaceful place again.

On the sidewalk a little girl with a yellow raincoat and rubber boots is playing in a puddle. A woman watches her from her balcony, signalling to her that it's all right. A sudden longing to be her age, have a mother who would focus her gaze on me. A mother like Mama before the tragedy.

Mama woke me up this morning. "Were you asleep?" I didn't dare answer yes, she would have apologized profusely. I was anxious to find out about her holiday. With the help of his wife, Anne, Philippe had managed to persuade her — the sea, a modern house where she'd have a beautiful room, and the grandchildren. Mama could go on forever on the subject of her grandchildren! Véronique, already five, her cuddles, her sandcastles. And Pascal, who was just beginning to talk. She mispronounced words to show me what he sounded like. She roared with laughter.

Then abruptly her voice broke. Did I remember? Noëlle had dug a deep hole in the sand, then the incoming tide had covered it up, she'd burst into tears. It all came back to me, how upset Noëlle had been and me not understanding.

I made an excuse, someone at the door, so I could hang up. I looked for a photo in my old album. Papa had taken a picture of us, Noëlle and me, spades and buckets in hand. Behind us, Mama, in her bathing-suit. She was knitting wool socks for the winter, which were always so warm in our boots, all the while keeping an eye on Philippe who was asleep on a blanket.

I couldn't find it. But that picture existed, I was sure of it — I hadn't just imagined it. I noticed how the lump was swelling in my chest, with the tide flooding holes in the sand, and lost photographs. That lump tells us things, about the past, how the past can be a lead weight if we haven't been able to grow accustomed to it. But we never become accustomed to someone's disappearance. We never do.

Chapter Eleven

I say "abandonment." I don't know why. And a vast desert stretches out before me, the sand gets into my nostrils, and the wind, the fabric of the wind wraps itself around me like a shroud. But Vincent answers, "future," and "hope." Now the park looks colourful again. A bird flies overhead, I would like to picture it as being blue — the bluebird, a sign of things to come. Only our imagination can save us from falling apart.

Over the surface of the pond tiny boats are gliding along. Children are steering them from a distance, they practise heading out to the open sea while their parents chat nearby. I try to overhear snatches of conversation but don't

manage very well. The city with its high-pitched noises
filters through the treetops.

Vincent. He is holding my hand very tightly in his and I
repeat the word "hope" just to myself. I am overcome all of a
sudden, overwhelmed to feel someone's warmth against me.

When he suggested we meet, I envisioned a contract of
the type one secretly dreams about, a gift. But here is his
hand on my palm and that is all I want now, his hand
holding mine. I walk along beside him in a daze. The
flower bed with the dark purple flowers, the clouds
banking up over our heads — nothing makes me gloomy
any more. I barely hear what he is explaining to me. Then
these words catch my ear: film script, a movie for
television. So my hunch had been right.

I withdraw my hand from his, move away from him a little
bit. My head is a maze, I must find the right answer. "Take all
the time you want to think it over." He tries to talk me into it.
How can I make him understand, I am in a place deserted by
language, language that is alive I mean, language that weeps
and dances and sings. I only feel at home with other people's
words, wouldn't he have an idea for a translation? But he
insists. He would like a text by me. That's what he really
wants, to work on a text that is a reflection of me.

Once again he reaches for my hand. That wonderful
warmth. My body remembers — the nights come back, the
glorious calm after the storm, murmured words. I lower my
eyes. I say yes.

The film script will open with the flight of a bluebird.

12

Chapter Twelve

Before, my soul sometimes became so light my body couldn't hold it back. It escaped and soared while I stayed behind, restrained by the gravity of the world, wondering where my soul would end up. I would look at even the humblest objects with fresh eyes: a chair needing to have its crossbars reattached, a faded lampshade, a romance novel.

You always knew how to sweep me up into that ordinary, reassuring kind of beauty. You would come up to me quietly, as a man does when he has loved a woman for a long time. You'd put your arms around my waist and I thought it was all very real, the celebration of our love. But I must have got everything mixed up, desire and love, love and routine.

And now desire is coming back, unexpectedly, like a dress lifting up in the wind. A hand on my palm was all it took to set me dreaming again of lips against my breasts. When I opened my eyes a little while ago, I imagined Vincent's broad fingers on my thighs. I gently stroked myself until the light exploded at the corner of the window. The dust particles whirled around, I could see the whole room, caught in that lovely disarray.

I liked that vision — desire creating infinite motion, the circle of time opening, and not crushing us. I went to get a writing tablet, a pen, and mauve ink. I settled myself in bed with lots of cushions.

I know nothing about my script, but I am going to start it right here in my bed with that very nothingness, so I might capture the precise moment when we come back to life, when loss is transformed into fiction.

Some day I will be able to describe your spicy smell without missing it. And the splendour of July, even in a narrow strip of garden.

13

Chapter Thirteen

"You really don't know where your husband is?"

I didn't answer. I stared at the living-room wall, without pictures, without a single poster, just the bare wall. In the alley-way we heard a dog barking and that made my silence almost acceptable. Your colleague was observing me discreetly from behind his horn-rimmed glasses, I sensed his disconcerted look. At the office, they were just as much in the dark as I was, but that didn't make me feel any better.

I detected a feeling of pity on his face, I couldn't bear it. "Get out," I screamed, pointing at the door like an actor in a school play. He was frightened, I think. He

snatched up his briefcase, forgetting his notebook. I heard
the door slam shut. I started to shake.

The day had slipped through my fingers. It left me
standing there in the middle of the living-room feeling as
bare as the wall in front of me. But then the room filled
up with police, all the policemen who had come in a
steady stream to our house after Noëlle disappeared.
They kept asking me questions, always the same ones,
while I tried to remember some detail, some small detail
— yes, Noëlle knew that man, he had been coming to the
recreation centre for several weeks, he was very
handsome, with a dusky complexion. Yes, they had
danced together several times, he held her close, she had
changed a little over the last weeks. No, I didn't notice
right away that she was gone, I was dancing too, with a
redheaded boy of my own age who looked ordinary next
to Noëlle's admirer. Didn't anyone find it suspicious that a
thirty-year-old man came to spend the evening with a
group of teenage girls?

Mama, in her armchair, with little bags under her
eyes, tried to cheer us up. Perhaps she had simply run
away — one fine morning Noëlle would turn up again,
tired of love bites on her neck.

But the police wouldn't let up. "Try to remember."
Once again the day came to a halt. I had to make an
effort to slip into my sister's life as I imagined it, the sweet
nothings they must have said to each other in the dance
hall's shadowy light, their hands lightly touching, and the
promises they must have made. I was Noëlle Villeray, a
stranger asked me to come with him. I didn't turn my
head toward my older sister who was dancing with a
redheaded boy, I pretended she wasn't watching me as I
walked out of the door. I melted into the night. And
girlhood closed like a book.

But I quickly returned to my own role, that of Emma
Villeray. My life story was weighing me down, I hadn't
learned how to forget. I hadn't. A scene flashed through
my mind in which I was waving. I was with Noëlle and

42   that stranger. And you. And a woman whose dim form
      appeared to me for the very first time. The São Paulo
      woman.
          I sat down. Everything around me was coming apart —
      that was another tragedy and yet a strange calm hung over
      things. I don't know why, but I felt deeply moved.

14

Chapter Fourteen

He wanted to see me. I asked Vincent if it was about the script. He said no, he just wanted to see me. My ear could make out the syllables but the sounds wouldn't turn into words. As when we are filled with fear. Fear caused by people running away and all the unanswered questions. I stroked the china cat you'd given me, I was trying to shield myself physically from him. He broke the silence. "Is seven o'clock all right then?" I hesitantly answered yes.

When I hung up I noticed the light on my desk, a sprinkling of small, white patches. They looked like daisy petals, as in that counting song, "I will be married, I won't be married, I will be a Sister." Noëlle had been puzzled by this

44 for a while. "A sister like you, Emma?" "No, Noëlle, a sister in black with a cross."

Iron cross, wooden cross. On Papa's tombstone in the cemetery Mama had had Noëlle's name inscribed with the date of her birth. One day, if her body were ever found, the inscription would be completed. I didn't believe it. In my mind there was a grave that would never be closed.

I opened the red notebook with the embroidered cover, the one I had found in an out-of-the-way shop and immediately marvelled at. On the first page, right in the middle, I wrote my name in capital letters, then "Noëlle," then your name. "Jérôme." I stared at it for a long time as it lay open and empty among the daisy petals and my good intentions. One day there really would have to be some certainties, even in a story that was obviously fictional, a story that would end with the dead neatly stowed away in coffins that were going to be covered up with earth and green grass. Good-looking corpses, embalmed, made up, draped in satin, who would be sleeping a different sleep from mine. For all eternity.

I turned the notebook over. On the last page I wrote, "The End." Some day my script would be finished. I wouldn't feel that I had to wear black any more.

Chapter Fifteen

I wish Vincent were here with me now. I wish he wouldn't come. I am waiting. Ahead of me looms an inexpressible reality and I am waiting. I don't know how far I will go yet. Perhaps beyond the limits of my self-control, where the heart begins to hammer against its cage, where I will do what he wants.

Nothing is happening at my neighbour's place. For the past few days nothing has stirred. The curtains stay closed, the garden is overgrown with weeds. Every now and then through the partition walls I think I hear sobbing intermingled with prayer. And I say to myself, perhaps one more tragedy in the city.

46   It's him. Vincent is here, his arms loaded up with
groceries — vegetables, cheeses, pâtés, wine. He wants us to
cook dinner together. Afterwards we can pick a show to go
to. The evening quietly settles into a pattern. I should feel
good about that. But a man is moving about, he walks
around the table, opens the refrigerator, takes out the
wooden salad bowl. For the first time in this house. He will
leave his fingerprints. Then those will be gradually covered
up with dirt, with oil from food. Or the fingerprints of
another man. One day, all these traces will be gone.

He caught the change in my smile, he would like a
simple answer. Yet there isn't anything I could tell him that
would fit. I shrug my shoulders as if to say, "Just ignore it,"
but he walks over to me. I look down. The words aren't
coming. They may only exist in the form of gestures —
taking his hand, holding it very tightly in mine. Then, with
my finger, tracing one by one the features of his face, the
eyes, the nose, the mouth, to make him feel my fear. Letting
him undo the buttons of my shirt and look at my breasts in
the slanting sunlight.

No, the words aren't coming when he takes me into the
bedroom. They won't come. We are in total silence, we
move toward a blind space, we enter into a ritual we will
have to relearn.

The bed receives me. It isn't the same bed I shared with
you. It is the same bed. The place of crucifixion, arms held
back by long nails driven into the flesh, the slow agony, then
a violent, devastating burst of life which shatters all the
symbols of death.

His hands on my breasts. Sliding down to my thighs.
His fingers. He licks me. We slowly become accustomed to
this unfamiliar truth — hands other than yours penetrating
my flesh. Broad patient fingers fighting your presence. I let
myself be ravaged. I am incapable of reacting. Burying my
nostrils in his armpits, gently running my index finger over
the tip of his sex, moving my mouth toward his skin.

My eyes blur with tears, I am waiting for death. Enter
me, go down deep inside me, take me, I want you so hard

it will make me scream, plough into me, mix your sperm with Vincent's, fill me up one last time. Then you will leave the bedroom. I won't turn around, I will be looking at Vincent — his body and yours will be separated, differentiated forever.

Vincent knows, we both know. "I think I am in love with you," he says, perhaps to reassure me. He places his hand over my mouth, he doesn't expect an answer. Not now.

16

Chapter Sixteen

A different city is coming in through the window today, a jumble of quiet, subdued, sanctified sounds. I don't know exactly what time it is, half past nine or ten. Vincent has just left, he had to meet someone. The empty place beside me takes up all the room, but the bed doesn't seem enormous. Its human dimensions have come back — its sweat, its delicate sperm patterns on the crimson sheets. I am sitting in a bed that looks as though it had never known any farewells.

On the wall in front of me characters file by, they obey a strange logic. The woman doesn't want to give her body, yet she opens it, offers it up, lets herself be violated. She experiences a joy she finds impossible to define. Someone has entered her. She is fighting a battle she doesn't want to win. That is exactly it, desire, agreeing to lose, a patch of blue in the night, a few stars which grief hasn't managed to blot out, small acts of courage.

The next day, we can't tell any more what part we play in the story, the light has shifted.

With you I could tell right away, but I am probably embellishing. You seemed so lost at that reception. Was it you who came up to me? Or me who came up to you? It doesn't matter — very quickly we met up together, and as we faced each other you murmured, "It's so rare." I nodded yes. I felt overwhelmed. All that needed to be said had been said, I was waiting for you to act. We got our coats. There was a snowstorm outside, cars were skidding. We walked as far as the river. Then we went back to my place, into the warmth, the half light, the soft blur of evening.

You didn't mention your wife. That evening Judith didn't exist for me yet. It didn't puzzle me that you wouldn't sleep in my bed, I didn't ask any questions. You said, "I'm going to leave," and you left; I drifted off to sleep, I had a dream, you were picking a lilac branch, you offered it to me. The moment I reached for it, it changed into a brooch which you pinned on my blouse.

I didn't have any dreams last night, at least not one like that. It took me forever to fall asleep. That is what I wanted, to hear the noises in the alley-way, to feel Vincent's breath on my cheek, to see the ceiling as a cloudy sky. And think of you. You must have been asleep in São Paulo. With that woman beside you. Does she know about me?

A few days later I had insisted. One night, one night together, why refuse me that? At first you didn't say anything. Then the words broke away from their block of silence and dropped down on me while I tried to protect myself from them. I heard, "My wife," then, "Étienne, still so small," and that old refrain, "I'm sorry, I'm so sorry." I turned around so you wouldn't see my face. The candles in my eyes had been blown out, but I wasn't crying. You somehow overcame my anger, somehow managed to convince me.

50   This love, our love, had taken you completely by surprise;
tact was needed — eight harmonious years after all with the
same woman.

I had to put up with the evenings alone, with time cut
up in small pieces. I accepted this. When you arrived at the
apartment one night a few months later with your luggage
and drafting boards, I was glad I had been patient.

Vincent hugged me very tightly before he left. In his
arms there emerged something more definite than promises
— a trust, spacious and joyful, a bright room where the sun
dances. A desire to let myself be carried along. I don't know
if I am right.

You are still asleep. The woman beside you is beautiful.
You haven't told her about us. Why should you, since I no
longer exist. You are sleeping. You are in São Paulo. I have
decided this is how it is. There are certain things I need to
feel sure about.

Chapter Seventeen

I try to believe the past doesn't exist, only a bright, rosy future that is ready to sweep us along. With Bénédicte I sometimes manage this, with real women friends one can. She strides along, waves her arms about, laughs as if she never missed anybody. As soon as her love affairs are finished, they are locked away in cupboards, she has no regrets. She cries for a bit, then gets over them. A new day begins — this seems to come naturally to her. She says, "We must remember Lot's wife."

In my own cupboards nothing is ever put away for good, the doors don't shut properly. There's always a little crack that lets me see what is on the other side.

The Monday after Noëlle disappeared, Bénédicte had walked over to my desk in class, placed a small blue envelope in front of my hands, then returned to her seat without saying anything. I tore open the envelope. On the sheet of paper inside there was a single sentence written in a bold script. "There's no question of your failing your exams, we'll study together." I turned toward her. She winked at me, then continued with her mathematical problems. In my mind I had pushed my grief a little bit aside, made some room for schoolbooks, exercise books, a dictionary. And Bénédicte.

I phoned her this morning. How about having a drink together in a bar later in the afternoon? She invited me over to her place — she had discovered a wonderful patisserie, we weren't going to cook. I wanted to tell her about Vincent. Not that I was worried, I wasn't. The feelings Bénédicte and Vincent had for each other were clear. But I felt it was necessary to let her know and be as truthful as possible. Already I was looking for a way of saying "Vincent and I" so that the sound of it might match the yet-so-fragile reality.

My window on the bus framed triplexes built before the war, stores selling cheap furniture, vacant lots, and gas stations. How many people, I wondered, spent their days in such an ugly setting? I looked away. In front of me, on the seat, someone had written with a marker, "Stéphane loves Nathalie." I smiled, I suddenly felt a wild adolescent urge. There was no one near me. I rummaged through my handbag for a felt pen and wrote, "Vincent and Emma." I contemplated my handiwork. The inscription was clearly visible, many people would read it.

I thought about the verb "to love." I hadn't been able to write it and yet it was the first verb I had learned to conjugate.

Bénédicte and I have our own rituals. Ever since our schooldays. We play different parts, we carry on: "This week's assignment, girls, will be to write five pages on Flaubert's phrase, *Madame Bovary, c'est moi!*" We tell each other about our joys, our little disasters and the bigger ones, about new beginnings, and when things go wrong we try to exorcise our demons. But I am not Bénédicte, she isn't me — her clothes don't fit me, neither do her solutions, just as mine don't fit *her*. That doesn't matter though. We'll joke, we'll pour ourselves another drink. And, amazingly, when the evening is over, a luminous rosy glow covers the darkness.

I talked about you, your favourite colours, the birthmark on your left shoulder, your fits of anger, the tone of your voice when you said, "I am leaving." And I went over all my theories: your spirit of adventure, a depression, that need of yours to take up new challenges, a secret illness perhaps, my resemblance to Judith, a fear of aging. And now another woman.

I never put into words the right questions — how desire is ignited, how it dies.

Bénédicte brought up the subject of Vincent. A flash of intuition or, rather, Vincent's silence a while ago when she told him about my break-up. At the party at her place she had noticed excitement in his bursts of laughter. I ventured, "Perhaps desire begins in the throat and then moves down to the heart." Bénédicte answered, "You are confusing love with desire again." Will I ever learn?

But she was very happy for me, and I'm sure she meant it. She said that Vincent wasn't at all like you. Right from the beginning, she had seen in your eyes that you would leave me. You had left Judith. Bénédicte believes that things have a way of repeating themselves, the seasons shadowing one another always in the same order — *that*, to her, is the law of the universe, God. Radical change doesn't happen in real life.

In front of us, on the table, our beer bottles were lined up just like all the other beers we had drunk together over the past twenty years, sitting at various tables. Also repeating itself was that glorious late-night giddiness, the waltz that for the last twenty years had had us swirling around in ever-widening circles.

54   I got up and put an old Strauss record on the turntable, I felt like waltzing. I was slightly tipsy, this was quite obvious to Bénédicte. But she put her hands around my waist. We hummed along with the music, we twisted around our steps — we wanted to store away in our memory chest a scene to hold on to forever.

second song

An Infinite Reservoir

Chapter One

He is an imaginary man. We are lulled by the waves, on the deck of a ship, and we see him drifting along on the surface of the ocean. On nights when blizzards rage he gets lost in the snow. He crashes down on a road and passers-by scream as they gather around. He is a corpse, yet he is laughing. But the sounds of his laughter fail to puncture the silence, they hang suspended by tiny strings above his body, they don't reach us. He will be the man in my script.

I picture a woman. In her hand, a stable world. She unfolds it, contemplates it, strokes it gently. And then it explodes, scattering ashes all over her face, masking her. For a moment she thinks she has been disfigured. She will be the man's wife, the woman in my script.

A little while ago I went down into the basement. For the second time. The throbbing at my temples wasn't quite so intense. I sat down on the dusty stairs with my red notebook. But only dim figures appeared. I drew a dead body, then another, until the page was filled up, always men, Monsieur Girard. I find it impossible to think of him as the former owner of this house.

Could it really be just a coincidence? I had never before met my neighbour on the street. I went up to her, introduced myself, and right away commented on her black dress, offered my condolences. She began to talk — her father had died, over there, in Mexico, she felt very sad. "Much cry much pray." Was there anything I could do to help? But she didn't listen, on and on she talked about her father, then she got to Monsieur Girard who had died too, and Madame Girard who'd also been so sad so sad. And in a kind of echo, I picked up "a shot" and "basement" and "the blood, the blood." Madame Girard had screamed so loudly she had heard it in her home through the poorly insulated walls. My neighbour didn't use the word "suicide," perhaps she didn't know the French for that.

The ground under my feet suddenly opened, there was nothing for me to hold on to, I was swallowed up. That mud in my mouth, that red, bloody mud. I stammered out an excuse and fled.

I took refuge in the living-room in front of the window. For a long time I sat motionless in the leather armchair, watching a black squirrel. He was burying his nuts in the lawn while images filed past him. Monsieur Girard, the revolver close to his temple. His index finger pressing the trigger. His skull exploding. The brain splatters in the dust. The thud of his dead body as it hits the ground. The tools which wouldn't be put away that night.

I don't know why I made the connection with Papa, *his* death, his heart which had gradually given out over the years, the operation his doctor convinced him to have. Didn't he

have many good years left to live? He hadn't been strong
enough to survive the surgery. "So worn-out for a sixty-seven-
year-old," the surgeon had said and, besides, Papa didn't want
to struggle any more. Since he retired, his memory had
caught up with him. Noëlle. Noëlle climbing onto his lap
when he came home from work, Noëlle whom he carried on
his shoulders on our walks in the park. Noëlle. His life was
behind him now, nothing could bring him back to us.

We weren't enough for him — how was I to accept
that? The first time I lightly skipped over the words as
though it were a game. In the beginning you don't really
believe it, but bit by bit the letters split away from one
another on your tongue, an acid froth appears which slides
down into your stomach. You go around with a burning
feeling inside — you walk and talk, but cannot accept that
you aren't good enough.

Mama would softly stroke Papa's cold cheeks, she'd
repeat that our misfortunes couldn't all be linked to Noëlle.
Papa had had such a hard life, a childhood without any
affection, the Depression, being poor, low pay, the war —
she managed to be reasonable about it. She cried, then dried
her tears. His heart was worn out, there was no need to look
anywhere else.

Whenever Mama says "worn-out heart," I hear "broken
heart." It all depends on how you see it. For Mama, life
pulsates in a red muscle which eventually runs out of steam.
As *I* see it, the heart fights against a treacherous ache that bit
by bit tears it apart. And nothing can ever mend it. "My
husband died from heart trouble," Madame Girard had
explained at the lawyer's office. Her lie was not really a lie.

I went down to the basement. I looked for Monsieur
Girard's heartache in the things that used to be his — the
workbench, the old tools, the fishing-tackle box. I hadn't
understood at the lawyer's why her son didn't want to keep
anything. I looked everywhere for Monsieur Girard but I
only found Papa.

The room smelled of ether. In a few minutes they would
come with the stretcher. Papa and I were alone. We looked

60   at each other for a long while without saying anything. Then I went up to him to stroke his hand. We could already hear the shrill whine of the saw in his ribs, the surgeon's terse commands. And he said to me, in that way men have who aren't good at talking, "You must try to forget." But Mama and Philippe came in so all I did was nod. I would try.

But I haven't been able to, no more than he was. In my life, the past forms tiny islands I swim around, sometimes until I'm utterly exhausted. But I'm swimming, not drowning.

I say "Émile" out loud. And my pulse speeds up. Monsieur Girard had the same first name as Papa — is that just a coincidence?

In my script the man will not have a first name.

Chapter Two

All parks look alike. One can see walkers trotting behind their dogs, others follow a ray of sunlight over the mountain. One also sees children on tricycles, parents who call them back when they stray too far away, a wildly fluttering kite on the topmost branch of an elm, fountains that perpetually spew out the same water.

When I was a child, I used to count my steps so I wouldn't lose them. Not any more. I am quite sure they sink into the ground along with the rain and grains of sand. I'm leaving my own invisible mark among things.

I pushed a strand of hair back in place. I was resolutely putting one foot in front of the other. In a few minutes I

62 would arrive at Madame Girard's. She wasn't expecting me, I hadn't let her know. How would I have explained my visit? How could I possibly have said, "I would like to talk to you about your husband's death"?

She gave me a warm welcome. In the living-room a book lay open on a coffee table, a beautiful gilt-edged book. I didn't ask what the title was, I was afraid of being indiscreet or, rather, of being disappointed. I wanted to remember that image of Madame Girard with a book in her hands. And next to that image I placed my own hands and all the books I had ever loved. Because the sharing of images leads to the sharing of secrets, I now felt able to tell her that I knew the truth. She appeared relieved. "Until I understand it, I'll have to keep it secret."

I almost cried out. Can we ever understand abandonment? I had my screechy voice, the one that fills space with bad vibrations. Anger was catching up with me here of all places, in the home of this defeated woman. Why? I was crying now, sobbing uncontrollably, crying — all that was unutterable poured out in my tears. Then Madame Girard came over to me and took me in her arms. I became a little girl again, I let her comfort me. She murmured, "We have to accept things even if we can't understand them." I was nestled against her bosom while she was addressing me as *vous*. I thought of Mama, of her arms, which since the tragedy could only open for her grandchildren.

The evening was changing the sky's texture. Tears always dry up in the end. Madame Girard relaxed her embrace and took me to her bedroom. In front of her bed she had put an oak bookcase full of beautiful bound volumes. She stretched out her hand to caress their leather covers. She recited, "Rome, Byzantium, Athens, Egypt, Mesopotamia." She was pointing to her books about ancient history with its rises and falls, unexpected turnabouts, conquests, invasions and frequent humiliations, black plagues, betrayals, cataclysms — all those things human beings had been forced to accept without understanding since the beginning of time. "There you have the infinite reservoir of memory," she said, *"memoria."* After that she fell silent.

She suggested I have dinner with her. I accepted. I accepted everything — the port, the ham, the city waiting for the night in the rectangle of the window as the woman in my script gradually became more distinct. She now had something to say: "We have to accept things even if we can't understand them." She said it in a hushed voice while stroking leather-bound books. To whom would she address it? To a woman. There are certain statements one can only make to a woman.

3

Chapter Three

It happened when we were having our dessert. Little Véronique had asked if she could go to play in the garden and Anne had said yes; my sister-in-law is a permissive mother. She would watch her through the window while sipping her tea. Overhead, the ceiling amplified the shrill creaking of the old wood — my brother Philippe was trying to lull Pascal to sleep. Each time, Mama promised to put a rug underneath the chair's rockers and then she'd forget. Behind the white tulle curtain, Véronique was putting on quite a show. I must confess that all three of us were admiring her, our eyes riveted on the pleated screen.

I didn't notice, at least not right away, that the air had

become lighter. Actually, nothing happened. I had picked up the porcelain cup from its saucer to bring it to my lips again and then, for a fraction of a second, my hand froze. I was startled. Véronique was running after the cat and I wasn't seeing Noëlle running after the cat. Every movement Véronique made erased Noëlle's form a little bit more.

I turned my head to check what Mama's silence contained, but it held only Véronique and, close to her, multicoloured flowers and raspberry bushes. This time I wasn't going to hear, "Do you remember Noëlle?"

I first thought it was because of the light — it settled evenly on things and shapes, so that each shape disappeared. Only splashes of colour were left, a vast streaked surface without any depth. I was trying to find a simple explanation, trying not to admit to myself that we never know why things change.

Philippe came downstairs. Pascal was babbling on in his bed, he would fall asleep eventually. In my brother's life, the days slipped quietly by — one would never have known that we spent nine months in the same womb. Anne is perhaps more like me. Philippe had pointed this out to me one evening, the same discreetness, the same reserve. Without any preliminaries, Anne began to speak, sounding rather solemn: "We are expecting another child."

Véronique became blurred, the scene had shifted. We exchanged kisses, good wishes, laughter. Mama brought out her book of crocheting patterns, she grew animated, she looked beautiful. And then she glanced at the clock — we had to tell François the news, how late was it there? She never could locate New York on the map. Then time stood still. The film jammed in the projector. The ghosts gathered once again around the table. Noëlle across from me, Papa at the end. François next to Philippe.

With her glasses on her nose, Mama was looking up the telephone number of her youngest child. Anne had gone out to join Véronique. Philippe stayed where he was, his arms crossed. He was staring at the swell of the teapot. He

66   probably saw children, lots of children, who could never
       make up, however, for past sorrows.
           To break the silence, I asked if they'd already chosen
       some names. No, they hadn't decided anything yet. As soon
       as they knew whether it was a boy or a girl, they would pick
       a living name, a name no one in the family had ever had. We
       looked at each other for a long time. And the empty places
       around the table became empty again.

Chapter Four

A hand, my left hand, and time unfolds. Chapped, with rings, bitten nails lingering on the tabletop, gestures composed even in their confusion. As soon as I slipped off my wedding band I noticed that my ring finger had shrunk below the joint. The skin had a white stripe. But perhaps my hand didn't look any barer than before.

I placed my wedding band on the right side of my life, where useless objects congregate — old keys, unscented letters, faded memories.

In the mirror, I drew a new face for myself, with catlike eyes, a strawberry red mouth. After that I did exercises using vowels, "a, o, u, i," as top models do. The mouth must be

68   held slightly open. When I say "o," I'm very alluring. You told me so.

You stood among the flowers in a dark suit. You showed me the coffin at the far end of the viewing-room. You asked me to lie down in it with my catlike eyes, my oval lips, you wanted to take a picture of me. You closed my eyes, brought my fingers together. It seems to me I heard, "Smile," then you pressed the shutter. A child cried out, "Mama, watch the birdie," and an egg hatched, a chick began to peep.

I woke up. Vincent was speaking to me. He had rung the bell, no answer, so he'd let himself in. We were going to be late for the concert. The concert? Wisps of satiny air entered my nostrils, filtered down into my chest. My heart wasn't hammering against that tight lump, it had plenty of room. I lay very still. I needed to return slowly to the light so I might bring back with me this comforted heart.

Was Vincent really keen on that recital? I lifted up the sheet, put my left, ringless, hand on my fur. Against the blackness, the stripe must have seemed even whiter. I said, "Take me." To feel his male sex thrusting into me, *his* sex, that fullness.

Beyond our moans a voice was heard. The woman next door had begun to sing on her balcony again and it was all linking up together — Vincent's kisses in my ear, my spasms, Madame Girard's books, and that egg breaking open. On top of dying embers I was lighting a new fire.

Chapter Five

A retired man arrived here this morning. "A good worker," Bénédicte had said, "you'll see." He is like Papa in the way he does things. The dishes are piled up on sheets in the dining-room, the house has shamelessly thrown off its clothes, it isn't mine any more.

I go upstairs, sit down at my desk, look up a synonym in the dictionary. Then I hear a cupboard being wrenched out and my pen makes a blotch on the paper. I see holes, and the rain coming in through those holes, and the cold, and the snow in a season that doesn't know how to hold on to the sun. So then I imagine a warm, empty space and on my sheet of paper I draw a kitchen with new cupboards. After

70 that I try to fit it into sentences. Not translate it, only see it light up among the letters.

Often I fail. I'll put down my writing-pad, make my way downstairs to check on the renovations. The workman looks amused when I appear. He must have recognized that anxiety on hundreds of faces. He explains the destruction, justifies it, sounding like a man who has no fear of winter. I listen to him and convince myself that everything's fine, everything's all right.

We may think we have become reconciled to our childhood, to the kitchen where our mother plodded on in her changeless life, but one day we begin to suffocate. It's not enough to open the windows, we need to drive out the ghosts, to keep ahead of the desire to run away. We hurry, we draw up plans.

I made lines with a marker and wrote measurements above them, as you used to do. Then with Bénédicte and Vincent I talked it all over, the realisation, the costs, the materials. I succeeded in hiding from myself that I was employing your vocabulary.

At first I didn't think about the destruction. That word came suddenly with the snap of the wood, like those baby teeth Mama would pull out of my mouth while Noëlle kept her palm clasped over her lips. When I woke up, I would find a silver coin under my pillow — I'd be able to buy chocolate. It all ended well, nobody dies from a trickle of blood. Mama taught us courage. One day we were going to be just like her, even look like her, supple and strong behind heavy stomachs which we would effortlessly carry around without toppling forward.

Mama has always refused to have her kitchen renovated. It's a kind of souvenir-album. Philippe tries to climb up on the table while François is getting his face all dirty in his high-chair. Noëlle grimaces, she hates green peas, and I? I've probably finished off my plate, I'm playing at being the oldest, I'm doing it well.

In *this* kitchen there were only imaginary memories. You, standing by the window so you could hear the neighbour sing; or sitting at the end of the table you chopped up vegetables. Images that flashed through my mind — you loomed up before me, you blended into the decor, then you disappeared. I would once again notice the cracks in the walls.

I've chosen colours that don't remind me of anything. Grey tiles, a dusty-pink countertop. I'll arrange a few mauve touches here and there, flowers whose name I don't know. I'm going to have a new ceiling lamp installed. I am dreaming up scenes that I like. Me, confident, free and easy with Vincent right beside me. Sometimes Bénédicte will come over for a meal, as will Madame Girard. I can see far ahead of me, I'm cracking my whip to spur on reality.

Chapter Six

The brilliancy of the light isn't the same here. Neither is the city's smell or its hum. Objects are cut off from their familiar exterior, they are too stark. How I dislike the anonymity of high-rises. But Vincent talked me into it, until the renovations are finished.

In the mornings I nestle down in bed with several pillows, work on my translation. Sometimes I take notes for my script, a word, a sulky look, a phrase that might propel my characters out of their own space and into the presence of each other's life story.

What could the woman have said to stop the man from committing suicide? I'm forever pondering that question without being able to come up with an answer. That is my tragedy, I mean, also my own tragedy — what could I have said to keep you from leaving? There has to be some word, some phrase, some facial expression with the power to prevent destruction, but where, I wonder, in the swarm of the days?

Madame Girard didn't agree, she clearly said so. She didn't sound like an old lady who was trying to put her mind at ease. Her husband would have killed himself anyway, she is convinced of that. No hidden keyword, no miracle. Even with regard to her son. When they grow up, children begin to revolve around their own sun, there is no way of keeping them. She swept her arm around in a circular motion that took in the whole place.

The tearoom was filled with people on their own, women, most of them elderly, who had abandoned their cramped apartments for an hour or so. The tablecloths struck me all of a sudden as being offensively rosy, as did the saccharine smile of the waitress and the soft music issuing from the ceiling. I felt like getting up and going over to people, but I just sat there, silently, in front of my cup. This must be what people call the *fin de siècle*. Women, each one at her own table, bringing their cups to their lips in time with the background music. Men somewhere else, but equally alone.

I definitely wasn't accepting anything. I almost said so, but Madame Girard had pulled some travel brochures out of her handbag, she wanted my advice, Rome or Greece? On a colour photo a man was smiling broadly. The *fin de siècle* had abruptly receded. Life was simple again — one only needed to look at this photo, picture oneself with that handsome, greying man, and one yearned for a change of scenery, wanted to be transported to Rome or Delphi and forget that the gods were long gone.

I suggested Greece rather than Italy, its skies as clear as the sea, the arid mountains. *That's* where I placed Madame Girard, in that bald and awe-inspiring landscape, so tranquil among the ruins.

74   "And what about you?" Some day. When I'd be able to look at destroyed temples without regret, without any nostalgia at all, when ruins would only mean a pile of stones that don't bleed, *then* I would, no doubt. But I didn't dare say so, I felt a little ashamed. I was comparing scars, mine and Madame Girard's — mine was certainly not as deep.

Madame Girard patted my hand, she was anxious to see the kitchen. She suggested we walk. We'd walk. The place had emptied. Only two women were left at a table by the window. They roared with laughter as they talked. I watched them for a long time, then took the arm offered to me and we disappeared into the crowds of people streaming out of offices.

While she was examining the cupboards, I copied down in my notebook this phrase — this exact phrase — of Madame Girard: "When I return from my trip, I will be able to go down into the basement again." Still, there was a slight quiver in her voice, it was barely noticeable, but I would translate it with the expression "no doubt." Madame Girard was trying to project herself into the future. Perhaps the future is also part of memory. Of *memoria*.

7

Chapter Seven

Every morning Vincent pulls the blind high up, like Mama.
He watches intently for the faintest glints of sun on the
mountain. Sometimes he steps out on the balcony to see
the city, a bird's eye view, from every angle, while I'm still
trying to open my eyes. I know that in a few minutes he'll
fold back my blankets and laughingly carry me into the
kitchen. Dear Bénédicte is expecting us in the country.
How lucky we are! It's beautiful out, will I promise to be
ready in half an hour? Yes I will. I will always promise. But
there you go. My head feels all foggy, we had too much to
drink last night, liqueurs after the wine, and then more
liqueurs. We talked so much.

76   He lies down beside me. Runs his hands over the curve of my hips. His sex hardens against my buttocks, I feel myself getting wet. This I know, this much I know — his desire for me, my desire for him, our bodies searching for one another in a space that is closer than words, even the densest, most passionate ones.

Elena. The name came up in our conversation between two sips of *crème de framboise*. Suddenly that mysterious shadow hung over us — Elena. An actress he had met on a co-production project, it was because of her he had gone to live in Rome. Three years of going back and forth between modern studios and a tiny, exorbitantly priced apartment not far from the Villa Borghese, mad love, hours spent waiting for her during performances, uncertainty when she was away. He unfolded before me an existence he hadn't spoken of to anyone, not even Bénédicte, an existence I couldn't begin to imagine. I must be too sensible. But Vincent said, "No, too uncompromising." To allow oneself to be drawn into the vortex of a passion, one needed to face right from the start that this passion was going to end.

He is moving gently in the small of my back. Never has he moved like this in her, Elena, I'm sure of it. With me it's a different kind of love. Different gestures. We don't moan every time as if it were the last, we find our way toward each other through repetition, a happy repetition that steadily burrows passageways under shifting ground. We are slowly fashioning a story and placing it beside our past stories which aren't totally forgotten though, since they revisit us late at night, in a pensive moment, in a strong brandy, or in the strains of a song.

Last night we snuggled up against each other and drifted into a heavy sleep while thinking about Elena. She was going to be part of my life from now on, follow me from a certain distance. Sometimes she would come nearer, so near I would almost be able to touch her. It wasn't jealousy or fear, only a kind of irritation. There are so many characters in a new love affair. And we can't do anything about it.

Chapter Eight

The unfinished furniture had been painted white, the old comforter with the dusty smell replaced with a pastel coverlet, and on a new bedside table, Bénédicte had put a bouquet of daisies, as in a country inn. I couldn't resist stretching out on the bed for a moment. The mattress wasn't lumpy any more, absolutely nothing had been overlooked. Then I drew back the window curtain so I might slip into the landscape, the greenery nearby, the lake that looked like all small lakes, and the mountain, set on the horizon. It was a scene that made one believe in eternity, in spite of the wear and tear on hearts, coverlets, and mattresses.

I left my travel bag in this room where I'd slept so many times when her parents were still there.

On the patio the red canvas deckchair, my favourite, was waiting for me. Vincent was sipping a Perrier and Bénédicte was teasing him, hadn't we spent countless nights solving the world's problems while soaking up unbelievable quantities of alcohol? Vincent was protesting, he hadn't got old, he was just tired. Since his return, he'd had to readjust — television was constantly evolving and, besides, it wasn't easy working for a private company. She listened to him without taking him seriously. Vincent detested her obsession with aging, she was well aware of that and unfailingly managed to get a rise out of him. I was witnessing a game, one of those games lovers play together long after their love has died, a moment's inattention during which their intimacy comes back to the surface.

I left my chair with the excuse I was getting myself something to drink and headed for the door. I felt uncomfortable, as if I were a *voyeuse*. Was Bénédicte trying to remind me, if only for a second, that she had been part of Vincent's life long before me? How I wished things could have been clear, feelings sharply separated from one another!

I superstitiously avoided the Perrier, poured myself a lemonade instead. I took a deep breath and went back. I watched summer racing over the lake, the murmuring water, the mountain lying in its own reflection. There was a lightness in the sadness, it seemed to hang from the clouds, it floated through the air.

"Is Madam lost in thought?" Vincent stroked the back of my neck, he was going to get drinks, would I like another lemonade? The past had dissolved. I was back in my usual place between him and Bénédicte. I didn't have to cope with that fear any more — me on my own, apart from them.

Bénédicte suggested we make a salad, so I had to come back to reality. Being hungry. Being thirsty. The physical world summed up in a few words that convey humanity's basic needs. And its infinite misery.

I chopped up the vegetables very finely, as though it

were a significant act. So many meals had been prepared in this kitchen, so many guests had gathered around the table of which we used to open out the side panels. Madame Lallier would fill the plates over the wood stove, Bénédicte and I were always ravenous, fishing at dawn in the rowboat it had taken us two days to repaint, swims, bicycle rides, hikes through the forest.

This is where my colour came back, the summer after Noëlle disappeared. And where Bénédicte told me a few years later about her and Vincent, that handsome young man she'd met at community television. I had held my breath for a fraction of a second, just long enough to search for some vague formula that would disguise my disappointment with good wishes for her happiness.

The sun was oppressively hot now. We needed to change the parasol's angle before settling down at the table, with pâtés and cheeses. Happiness was back, completely, without any nostalgia. The conversation started up again, but it was a different conversation, more sober, closer to the real weight of things and emotions.

We didn't speak about Elena, she was still too near us. We listened to Bénédicte — she candidly confided in us her hopes, her occasional loneliness, and the future. And then this phrase dropped among the dirty plates, wineglasses and sunshine, "I'm in love. With an extraordinary woman."

Dazed, Vincent put down his glass of wine. Bénédicte burst out laughing, pleased with the effect she had created, she was having fun. All I could muster was a forced smile. The mountain began to tilt, with its caverns, witches and dwarfs. Like the evening when Mama had shown me that squalling thing in the cradle that was called Noëlle. Once again childhood was lying in wait behind the summer heat, the smell of the breeze, the slightest word. All-powerful childhood.

But Vincent pulled himself together and proposed a toast. The three of us would never leave one another, come what may. Gently he rubbed his glass against mine. He was smiling at me, and thousands of smiles began to dance on the quietly glittering water.

9

Chapter Nine

We would drive Madame Girard to the airport. She had come right out and asked me to do this. After all, hadn't Greece been my idea? On the table she opened out a new map, just as new as the kitchen. Vincent and I had rushed to put everything back in its place so we might share our first meal with her in this space which was now clear of the past.

Madame Girard was as excited as a child. Together we followed the itinerary she had planned, we made the names of the cities ring out: Athens, Delphi, Mycenae and Agamemnon's tomb, Heracleion. She must see Crete, Vincent insisted, the Minotaur's labyrinth, the gorge of Samaria.

The gorge of Samaria. I liked the resonance of that,

solemn, mysterious — it seemed to me one could hide out forever in that narrow passage, that river of stones between cliffs. One day I would see the gorge of Samaria, I would see Crete. Before Brazil, before São Paulo.

I thought of you all the way to the airport. How long had I stayed closeted in the apartment after you left, I wondered. For ages, it seemed. I had come out of it with wrinkles and tiny red pouches under my eyes. And yet here was Madame Girard telling me while we were chatting a moment ago that I'd been looking younger lately. I shouldn't completely believe her, but even so I wanted to think my face was intact.

We left the luggage at the airline check-in counter. Fascinated, we looked around us, observing all those people arriving from nowhere. We let ourselves be soothed by the angelic voice issuing last calls for boarding.

"Does your mother like airports?" Madame Girard was asking a perfectly harmless question, but how should I answer? Mama couldn't bear departures — she had only set foot in here once, when Anne and Philippe came back from Zaïre after they'd been away for two years. She had waited in her Sunday best, her eyes riveted on the glass partition. She first saw Anne, and behind her Philippe, who immediately held up a small bundle wrapped in a white blanket. Mama laid her hand over her heart, I thought she was going to faint. When she received Véronique in her arms, tears flowed from her eyes. Life had just resurfaced.

She had come out of her grief. She began to dye her hair ash-blond, she was swept along by love. She called me "my big girl." Wasn't I her only girl now, her only surviving daughter? Every once in a while she asked my advice but, without listening to me, she would start up about Véronique again. And now about Pascal. Why blame her? She hadn't been consumed by her sorrow, that's all that mattered.

Already passengers leaving for Athens were asked to go to the departure gate. Madame Girard blew us a last kiss before she disappeared. But it wasn't a farewell kiss, I didn't feel sad, just energized. I felt like going away myself, what was really keeping me in Montreal?

82   "Next year we'll go away too." I said this in the tone we use when we try to sound more convinced than we really are. A tone that leaves no room for doubt. A tone that assumes there are guardian angels, roads bordered with daisies and sheep, altars on which to place our hands.

10

Chapter Ten

I didn't recognize her. More youthful than ten years ago, her hair cut short, in jeans, Judith didn't look like your ex-wife any more. She spontaneously came up to me, what a coincidence meeting at the movies. The tight lump in my chest returned, but Judith put my mind at ease right away, she simply wanted to ask me if I had heard from you. They hadn't. And her son hadn't got over it. She didn't refer to Étienne as *your* son, I noticed.

Silence drifted up through the ringing of the cash register and the popping of corn. I had to say something though. What slipped out was precisely what I wish I had kept to myself, "I just can't understand." But I immediately

84   checked myself — how much sympathy could I expect from this woman? In a humorous kind of way I forced out the words: "I'm going to steal away like a thief in the night." We looked at each other. Then I made some excuse and hurried away. Everything had been said.

On the giant screen Juliette Binoche mourned for her husband and their daughter. However wide I opened my eyes, each scene blended into other, by now almost unreal scenes. The cake I had baked for Étienne's birthday with its seven candles, the holiday by the sea, the death of the cat, his little-boy tears. Then, after you left, a teenage tantrum just like your fits of rage. All the blame fell on me, I hadn't been able to stop you from leaving. Étienne had started to turn down my invitations without any pretext. His stubborn silence in the receiver.

Finally the day comes when one realizes it is a long time since the last phone call. Love has been left in a screened-off part of the heart. In a year, or maybe ten years, we'll run into one another in a restaurant or at the movies. Only, we can't foresee the particulars. Judith approaching me some night, for example, with sentences full of gaps; Étienne hasn't got over your being gone. Was that an implied request? I turned the sentence over and over in my mind but couldn't figure out what to make of it. Did she want me to phone her son again, to keep on trying to breach the silence? One thing I was sure of though — she didn't pity me.

The movie suddenly chased away Judith's voice. By a combination of circumstances, Juliette Binoche met her husband's mistress. She learnt the truth and, surprisingly, the shock set her free. Now she too could begin to love again. She no longer needed to safeguard a glorious memory.

Perhaps this was what I needed, a great jolt, a collapse so terrible I would summon up whatever strength I had left to dig a passageway back to the light. I thought, if you'd left me for someone else that would have killed me, but maybe I would have preferred a lightning-quick death to being torn apart like this.

I left before the end. I needed some air, I couldn't take the darkness any more. Also, I didn't want to run into Judith again — I had a hunch I shouldn't push my luck.

I thought of the film's story as plausible.

11

Chapter Eleven

It seems I smiled in my sleep a moment ago. Vincent saw me spreading my lips, slowly at first, then I showed little tips of teeth — it was a genuine smile. I woke up with a beautiful image in my mind. A house full of windows like the ones I drew when I was a little girl and, right in the middle, a mouth, a red, happy mouth which was opening.

"Glad to be back in your own place?" Oh yes. Since the renovations, the house reflects me. I have washed all the windows, hung the pictures. Now the walls are vibrant. Together with Vincent I cleaned the basement. We destroyed the spider webs, sorted out Monsieur Girard's tools, washed the cement floor. Life is once again a more powerful word than death.

We don't know how we reach the turning point. Nothing definite happens, but imperceptibly our gaze shifts and we get moving again. We open our doors — we are surprised by noises we hadn't noticed yet, the squeaking of an old tricycle or a clothes line, exclamations in a musical language whose nuances we try to catch. We take a chance and admit, "It's lovely." Beauty suddenly steps out of the museums and the operas. It slips ahead of us, it follows us, it wraps itself around things.

I let myself be swept along. Really! Such enthusiasm over the first cup of coffee! Vincent set his cup down on the floor beside the bed, then he hugged me. He meant to say, I love you, you're beautiful, life has returned to normal or you have new hope. Perhaps even more, a diffuse kind of faith which it was still too early to express directly. Language can sometimes be so rough all it manages to do is frighten us.

He hadn't mentioned Elena again, I hadn't asked him anything. By being too intent on remembering those who are absent, we end up turning them into an evil force — they foist themselves on us, they interfere, they haunt us. Elena was part of a story that was dead, we needed to let her rest in peace.

In Vincent's caresses there was a passionate wish to create a place for us among the ruins. One day he would come to live here with me. In our house. We would have a garden with tulips and lilies of the valley. One day I would be done with deciding between the joys and the heartaches that are crammed into each object. But I'm probably mistaken. We dream new dreams before the last regrets have faded away. Today, I smiled in my sleep. It wasn't you who told me, it was another man and I believed him.

12

Chapter Twelve

I pretended I was writing about a woman I hardly knew. I described her timid-little-girl face, her eyes suddenly becoming veiled as she puts her left hand in front of her mouth to protect herself or stifle a scream. I reread my page out loud and tore it up — that character was not going to be in my script.

How was I to introduce Mama into my script? How could I write, "Mama is a disappointed little girl"? It's not because of Noëlle, it goes back a long, long way to a distant past which I guess I'll never know anything about. For the first time today I saw the shadow of an older life when the veil came down in front of her eyes.

On the radio a new recording of Vivaldi's *Four Seasons* was playing when the doorbell rang, two brief rings only. I hesitated. I was rereading the last chapter of my translation. It was a moment of grace, I had the impression that I had succeeded in preserving the other language in my own language, it seemed that nothing essential had been lost, neither the resonance nor the rhythm. Even so, I went to the door. A grey form stood with its back to me, still straight but huddled up. I felt a twinge in my stomach.

She put her bag down in the hall. She was on her way home from the doctor's, a routine visit, she quickly explained; she'd decided to come and see my renovations. She needed a pretext. She wouldn't have been able to say, "I just felt like seeing you." She doesn't know such words. "You have a very nice kitchen," she exclaimed. Sometimes all she can think of is trite phrases. I replied with an inconsequential remark. So there we were, making conversation.

I spread the linen tablecloth embroidered by Grandmama over the table. And right then and there childhood re-emerged through her wrinkles, the whole of her childhood, the dark curtain in front of the eyes, the hand over the mouth as a gesture of terror. That tablecloth at ten o'clock in the morning? I had just committed a treacherous act, Grandmama wasn't going to forgive us.

We don't know how connections between events are forged, how a face may carry within itself another face, a fear another fear, a mother her daughter. In Mama's eyes I saw Noëlle's fragility, her dread of the rain, of the neighbour's dog, of the messiness of our bedroom. In Mama's eyes I saw Noëlle's disappearance.

How old was Mama when she left her parents' home? Oddly enough, I had never asked her. "Seventeen." I repeated, "Seventeen, just like Noëlle." Mama gave me a searching gaze, then she looked down. The silence was heavier than lead. Finally she spoke. Noëlle hadn't been abducted against her wishes, she was sure of it; she had carefully prepared her escape.

Mama said what I had never dared to admit plainly to

90   myself. I began to breathe again. We had no idea what had
       happened next, but at least there was this tiny bit of
       certainty — Noëlle had gone with that handsome stranger
       of her own free will.
           "I hope God will forgive me." The phrase escaped from
       her mouth like a moan. I asked her why. "I don't know how
       to hold on to my children."
           I went over to the window. A Boeing pierced the rainy
       sky. I suddenly felt like going away. I said, "You've managed
       to hold on to *me*." But Mama didn't hear, she was shut away
       in some remote spot deep inside herself. Where I had never
       been able to reach her.

13

Chapter Thirteen

"By night the avenue resembles a dark tunnel leading nowhere."

I agree. I always agree when Vincent describes the city with images as real as those in a film. I'm amazed every time. My own images stick to my skin, they don't belong to the order of visible things, they first appear as patches smelling of lilacs or bleach, but after that they become clear, they end up forming strange landscapes that exist only in books.

Vincent and I see things differently. But when I'm worried, I agree as if I were touching his hand. Then everything goes back to being simple — I find him again. I

92   catch my breath, I'm twelve years old. Some day I'll have to grow up, but I don't know how one does that.

With you, I never asked myself the question. The seasons slipped by and as we watched them we were oblivious to time, oblivious to the lines of time on our faces. But on your birthday you declared, grimacing, "I'm now in my fifties. What a horrible thought!" You were unenthusiastic at the party we had for you, with a cake and candles. Your son had been saving up so he could buy you a silk dressing-gown. You barely murmured, "Thank you, Étienne." You weren't with us.

I didn't notice right away. I had convinced myself that you would eventually get used to it. But our life had just tipped over.

It's frightening to think that I didn't notice. That every little fact stayed isolated from other little facts, on its own small island. You no longer talked about our next vacation, didn't renew your subscription to the opera, you didn't cook any more. Little by little these events link up with one another, they make up a plausible chain.

We've arrived. It's impossible to park in front of the house. We have to drive around the block. Together we look for a space in the night, scanning both sides of the dark streets. I signal with my right hand, I've found a spot.

I get out. The street stretching out ahead of me resembles a long, dark tunnel. This time *I* say it. It isn't an image any more, but a sensation that races up my spine, spills over into my eyes, lifts up my cheeks in a great surge of happiness. We are together and I can see. We still have to walk back up the tunnel. It will end in my bedroom, in the hollow of my bed. There the night will lie down, captive. And at ease.

14

Chapter Fourteen

A new postman came by this morning, a jolly young man with an athletic build, a student probably — I couldn't imagine him bringing anyone bad news. He rang, dropped off a pile of envelopes: letters, magazines, flyers. He asked had I ever considered installing a larger mailbox. I promised I would think about it and, amused, I closed the door. My old postman wouldn't have been as direct. A matter of age, or a matter of being of a different generation.

I took a quick look, nothing important, and went back to my desk. Then the troubling fact struck me — not for a moment had I been hoping for a letter from you. I scrawled the date in red on the calendar on the notice board. Facing

94   me, a girl had been sitting on a swing since the beginning of
the month, with the tranquil expression of someone who
had never known any unhappiness. For the first time, I didn't
envy her. I didn't hold it against Renoir.

How does one escape from the months of waiting,
through what gap in the hard wall of time? Once we're on
the outside, we turn around to glance back with the
awareness of another time, a spongy, springy one which no
longer confines us. I stopped working. It so happened I
needed to go over to Madame Girard's to water her plants.

The light drifted over green lawns, across already warm
sidewalks, lingered over the pond in the park, a rich, ochre
light which I hurried after. I would hide out at Madame
Girard's in the privacy of her apartment, I would rebuild a
beautiful world from a fragment that hadn't belonged to you.

I stopped at the patisserie, bought some crab mousse,
which you used to find insipid, and a stick of whole-wheat
bread. The present would push old worn time out of the way.

I talked softly to the plants, cleaned their leaves, stroked
them so they would keep themselves alive. Then I put on
some music and had a picnic with the crab and the whole-
wheat bread in a rectangle of light on the tiny balcony. A bit
of earth remained stuck under my fingernails. Never mind. I
was hungry, I was thirsty, a summer thirst — I would have
another glass of wine, a summer wine. I pulled my skirt up
over my thighs so I might be a woman with summer legs.

The city began to tilt ever so slightly, just enough that
in the distance, above the river, I could make out bodies in
the midst of taking flight. They weren't angels, they were
only ordinary human beings finding a place for themselves
in the radiant sky.

Chapter Fifteen

I took a deep breath and the moment expanded. It covered us, it was a soft, fragrant bubble where we were together again and could confide in each other.

"I'm afraid of losing you." This is all I said, seven syllables suspended above me in empty space, which could come crashing down on the table between us. Bénédicte parted her lips, was I jealous? I shook my head, I wasn't, but I feared being abandoned. Forgotten.

The lump sat in my throat. It came with the word "forgotten." Confessing this had pitched me once more into a void without form, a bottomless pit. A tear rolled down to the tip of one of my eyelashes, another little bit of sorrow having made its way through my eyes. I swallowed. The terrace was packed, personalities from the world of journalism, was this the time to make a spectacle of myself?

An old woman went around the tables begging for money, muttering in some Slavic language. I was unable to take my eyes off her ragged clothes. She was about to come up to us, I felt strangely ashamed. I held out a few coins to her while turning my eyes away from her gaze. That woman was like me, wasn't I also begging for something?

Since our weekend in the country I hadn't heard from Bénédicte. She always reacted in the same way when she was in love, she was off on a desert island, violins playing. But eventually life went back to normal — work, our friendship — we were having a meal together today, weren't we? So why was I worried?

The old woman now shuffled across the boulevard. With every step she took I was afraid she would be hit by a car. She really was the figure of doom.

I asked Bénédicte to tell me about her lover, June, so I might get used to her silent presence, take her into our space. I waited. The words fitted together in the usual way, they drew a portrait I would barely remember. That woman didn't interest me since I could go on saying, "Bénédicte and me." Since that stood for a reality rooted in the past.

We had our liqueurs on the terrace of the restaurant next door. The lump in my throat dissolved in the brandy. In the breeze tickling my shoulders. In the tender look in Bénédicte's eyes. In another liqueur at another equally trendy restaurant where the waiters wore suits from the fifties. Then in this confession from Bénédicte: "I've been afraid of losing you, too." Now everything had been said.

We fell silent. The sun couldn't hold its own against the breeze any more. I shivered. I put my sweater back on without complaining that autumn was already moving in on us. Or that the two of us had to part soon. Bénédicte was going back to June, I would join Vincent. We would have dinner with them, we'd make love, we'd sleep together.

Maybe they would ask us why we were suddenly so calm, but we wouldn't answer. How were we to tell them that we had confronted our deepest fear today and conquered it, until the next time?

16

Chapter Sixteen

Too much noise, too many people on the street. Too much city for one pair of eyes. It's Friday. Summer, office closing time, bursts of laughter, cracks in the mind allowing glimpses of a blue lake, of an amorous embrace. What is Bénédicte doing now? And Vincent?

Suddenly you are there, on the sidewalk across the street. You smile at the woman close to you. *With* you. She is gorgeous. Ebony skin. The way she walks. You take her hand. You decide to cross, you twist your way through the traffic. Which is waiting for the green light. With her. *Her.* She smiles, a lovely smile. You are coming toward me, you are both coming toward me. My chest. My heart. I must lean against something. Anything at all. Quickly. I've got to escape. Dash into a store. Too late. Your eyes are going to meet mine, your eyes meet mine.

It isn't you. Obviously I had too much to drink.

Sweat runs down between my shoulder blades, my dress is soaked through. My legs are like rubber. Such throbbing at my temples, I'm hot, I'm cold. I have to sit down for a few minutes on this bench. Calm down a little. Where am I? Five minutes away from Vincent's. I'm saved. If I don't get up soon I'll be slumped on this bench till nightfall. I've got to hail a cab. My legs are shaking but they're holding me up.

I give the address, then go totally blank. I shut my eyes, I have no thoughts. I don't want to think. The city falls away, the noise, the people, it's all gone. I'm there. I pay the driver. Never mind the receipt.

A neighbour is standing near the elevator. "You look awfully pale." I nod at her. No need to worry, I'm fine.

I ring. No answer. Vincent isn't home yet, I take out my keys. There is a note on the table. "Back around seven. See you then, my love."

My love. Tears come streaming down my face. My love. A warm tongue in my mouth. A lollipop. Vincent. I roll myself up into a ball in the bed amid our night smells.

17

Chapter Seventeen

Nothing filters through. The day is opaque, a heavy curtain drawn shut. I watch myself stirring with my inner eyes, the ones that remember my shattered body, each fibre, each nerve of my paralysed hands.

When Vincent returned last night, I just had to explain. I told him — the man on the sidewalk, the beautiful woman he was with, their love. The mistake I made, my collapse. I chose the truth, I wouldn't have been able to lie. After a short silence he murmured that he understood. I understood too. For a few seconds he saw Elena. With another man.

We spent the evening in bed. Ate in bed, talked in bed. Then we pressed ourselves against each other and fell asleep. We didn't make love, our gestures would have been too remote.

This morning you are gone. Vincent is sleeping peacefully. What has he done with Elena, I wonder. I get up, plant a kiss on his cheek, quietly close the bedroom door behind me. Only a cheerless light seeps into the kitchen at this hour. I fill the coffee-maker reservoir, put in the filter, count the spoonfuls — one, two, three, four, five, six — I split every minute up into its basic parts so as to reconstruct the present.

The coffee will be ready soon. Vincent will stretch out his arms to me, I'll whisper words of love to him and the bedroom will fill with promises again. We'll leaf through the big atlas and conjure up rivers of diamonds, enchanted forests, friendly spirits. We'll pretend we're far away, far enough away that memory won't be able to find us.

One day you will be an indistinct figure on a distant shore. All I need do is wait. It's a matter of patience.

Vincent's voice, Vincent's presence. Once again life softens the shadows. I pull up the blind, carry in the first cup of coffee. What will we do today? He is trying to think of something a little bit crazy. How about driving into the country without planning where we are going? Picking a road at random, arriving at some inn or a pretty hotel or an awful motel, renting a room there, taking photos of ourselves, lots of photos which we'll have developed when we get back — by a lake, next to a group of trees, in front of a window, or by the edge of a swimming-pool? What time is it?

Vincent is gathering up his things, we'll stop by the house to collect some clothes. The city opens up through the window, the clouds in the sky are as frothy as the milk on top of our coffee, our kisses will taste of cinnamon, they will leave foamy traces around our lips. Today will be a reprieve.

18

Chapter Eighteen

All I want is to be encaged by someone's body. Two arms hugging me, hands on my buttocks, only this, gestures more truthful than words, and the quiet lapping of water against the shore. Hold me tightly and chase my nightmares away. I drift into a sleep as gentle as the lake, as tranquil as the pale shade of pink of our room, "Country-inn pink," Vincent commented as he set down our luggage.

He is asleep. Every breath he takes reaches down to my very core. Vincent will be my guardian angel. He knows how to untangle hopes and regrets, his feet aren't stuck in things from the past. At noon he asked a woman to take a photograph of us at the service-centre picnic table. The wind was blowing my hair in front of my eyes, but he wanted a memento, right then and there, beside the cafeteria.

"In our old age we'll say, 'We were there.'" He can see far into the future, too far for me as yet, but I like the assured way he says "our." He pulls me into his world which is filled with simple things, with wild raspberries appearing every summer, birds that faithfully come back to their nests, small out-of-the-way hotels where there's always a bed left. Here, we got the last room. Modest but clean. Cosy. Not for one moment did he have any doubts about us finding a place to stay. Despite the bright sunshine, the summer holidays, the profusion of American licence plates on the road.

Confidence is a strange phenomenon. His confidence is as vast as the night, mine breaks at the slightest jolt. It's only skin deep. Ghosts lurk at the heart of my joys, that is my little tragedy. But not just mine.

This never struck me in Philippe. My brother is a handsome man. "He looks like Uncle Jean," Mama always says — his build, the dimple in his chin, a kind of natural distinction. Also, he has a good job with an international development agency. People fly in from all over the world to meet with him. He travels a lot, has a stable life. It seems unthinkable that when life veers out of control he might be upset by it.

One night Anne and I were singing with Véronique while we pointed out the farm animals in her new picture book. She was rubbing her eyes. In a few minutes she would fall asleep on the sofa and I'd carry her up to her bedroom, the bedroom of a doted-on little girl.

But Philippe's car came to a stop in the driveway. Véronique jumped up to go and welcome him, she was now completely awake. Anne and I looked at each other, our strategy had just failed. Philippe appeared, all smiles, with his daughter in his arms. He told her what he had done during the day, pulled an illustrated book about an African country out of his leather briefcase. She settled herself on his lap to turn the pages one by one while asking lots of

104   questions so she wouldn't have to go to bed yet. Philippe
acted as if he didn't notice. He explained each photo in
detail — it was a touching sight, Véronique's chestnut curls
against his black beard.

I closed my eyes for a moment to search my memory for
a scene like this one with Papa, but nothing came. Only our
three story books with their old-fashioned drawings of
madonna-like fairies, the voice of Mama, so tired at times,
and Noëlle invariably asking, "Where Papa?" Papa hadn't
come home yet, he was working overtime. Mama had
resigned herself to that. Carriages kept on changing into
pumpkins and princes into frogs, as together with her we
stepped into a happy world, full of children.

Anne was swelling up like a balloon. "I can feel the baby
moving already," she said, laying her hands over her
stomach. Philippe beamed at her. That is what they both
wanted more than anything — her womb spilling out in a
few months' time into a cradle. "We are going to fill our
home with children." Véronique clapped her hands. Did she
understand what Philippe was saying? It doesn't matter, she
shared her father's magical belief in a house without cracks.

I shuddered. Somewhere in my mind a tiny boy was
clapping his hands. Papa had come home earlier that evening.
Mama wouldn't be telling the Cinderella story for the
hundredth time. We had our Papa all to ourselves. He was
going to build us tractors with the meccano set, houses from
small red bricks, solid structures that weren't likely to collapse.

Vincent is dreaming, he pronounces my name, holds me
even closer. I fight off sleep, I don't feel like sleeping. I stay
awake and keep watch, nestled against my guardian angel.

Third
Song

Ariadne's Clew

1

Chapter One

A bolt from the blue. Yet another one, is what I said to myself.

François phoned from New York. My little brother is coming back. Could he stay at my place while he looks for an apartment? Why at my place, why not at Mama's or Philippe's? It's a mystery to me. François is a chip off the old block, he's so tight-lipped. One has to guess what's on his mind. I thought of the children at Anne and Philippe's. I thought of the torrent of love that would wash over him at Mama's, he wouldn't be able to move. That was a good enough answer for me. I had many other things to take care of. Where was he going to sleep, for example? I wandered all through the house, examined the various possibilities, the

108 living-room, my study, the room where your boxes are piled up. I opted for my study, I would reorganize it, buy a sofa bed. François would be comfortable there. Also, my study was going to look like a small boudoir.

I hushed my doubts. Deep down I was annoyed at myself. When would I finally be willing to get rid of your things?

I didn't ask François if I could tell Mama the news. I decided I wasn't going to say anything. We would save the surprise for when François had actually arrived in Montreal; she had to be protected against reversals of fortune. What if François changed his plans? I need a great deal of evidence before I can believe anything, I have to be able to plunge my fingers into really deep holes. So I wait while pretending not to wait, I am hopeful but wary at the same time.

This past night you phoned me from New York, you told me you were coming back. I said all right, my lips tensing a little with worry — would the bed be big enough for the three of us, François, you, and me? But Vincent turned over and I woke up. Around me the darkness looked faintly transparent. Daybreak was near, I came back to reality.

During the night we confuse everything — what people mean, what men do, their casual way of saying, "I'm leaving" or "I'm coming back." As for François, he waited for a lilac-scented day in spring. He turned nineteen that Sunday and we had all gathered together, happy birthday François. He blew out the candles and in the same breath told us he was going away. He had found work out west in the oil fields, he would get to see the country, it would be an adventure.

Mama ran into the kitchen, Papa followed her. The three of us, Philippe, François and I, just sat there around the table. We didn't know how to react. The house would be a little bit more deserted, Mama a little bit sadder. For Philippe and me, the world would weigh a bit more heavily on our shoulders.

But Papa returned with a bottle of brandy. He approved of François's decision. He was proud of his son. Philippe relaxed, he proposed a toast. Papa had just allowed him to leave as well. Mama did her best to dry her tears, she poured coffee into our cups and I didn't know any more what to drink first, the coffee or the brandy. The words "I'm leaving" were stuck in my throat.

François is coming back. What that phrase really means just won't sink in — a lot of luggage, the occasional hint of an English accent in his French, curly hair, Papa's way of walking. François is coming back and I feel a shiver running down my spine, I'm afraid of black cats, broken mirrors, telephone calls at two in the morning, ambulance sirens. We had grown used to him not being here, we no longer expected anything from him.

Why is François coming back? Why am I not putting him in the room where your things are stacked up? That is the real question, the question of my grieving. But I don't have the answer right now.

2
Chapter Two

Stored among my memories are Grandmama's bent back, that party for my first communion, two or three stray cats, a goldfish, but no birds, no birds at all.

When I was a child I didn't know how to draw wings, songbirds had pigeon wings and pigeons had sparrow wings. Even the angels couldn't fly away. So I would sit them down at the foot of a bed. I made feathers for them with glints of delicate gold, eyes as pale as Noëlle's. Mama's eyes are earth-coloured, it would have been impossible to draw her as an angel. She belongs to the human race which coughs, hiccups, bustles about, and has hands of flesh.

She phones me every day now, for no particular reason,

she says, just to chat. What am I doing? Did I really need
that new sofa bed? She senses things, she is good at asking
the right questions and I still can't lie to her. But I'm resisting
as though I'd never learned to detect certain inflections. I
sidestep her questions. A minute ago I described the flower
pattern on the sofa bed to her and she asked me if I was
feeling all right. By constantly changing the subject I'm
making her worried.

I'm trying to take up my old position at my desk.
Where I sat before. Before my life was torn into two
unrelated parts. Now, out of the corner of my eye as I'm
hunched over the dictionaries, I catch a glimpse of the sofa
bed's dazzling colours. I can see the eighth card of the
tarot, the seated woman holding gold scales, and I think
about François's homecoming — it looks like I'm becoming
a better judge of things.

My translation is finished. Even the revising of the
revisions. I am fingering the manuscript in front of me, a
good two hundred and fifty pages which, in the fall, will
wind up between laminated covers with my name
underneath the title. There it is, it's all done, I feel relieved.
Time is slowly knitting together, I recognize my old self
again. I mean, here at my desk I am not everywhere at the
same time any more. There are walls and windows,
dictionary entries, synonyms which may not be perfect
substitutes but we use anyway to avoid certain clumsy
repetitions. There is the distance I cover between the door
and my padded chair, and all those countries that some day
I'm going to see from the window of an airplane.

"Grief expands our world," Bénédicte said.

She dropped by for an hour, just long enough to have a
cup of tea with me before going off to interview someone a
few streets away, on the subject of grief, it so happened.
When we are in pain, she explained, the universe no longer
has any boundaries, we live at the same time in the sky and
on the earth, in the North and the South, the forest and the
city. It's true, we aren't held down on the ground by gravity
— all lives are possible, everything, perfection is within

112   reach. But we are flesh and blood and sooner or later we need to be held down by someone's arms, protected by a roof, surrounded by books and friendships. We spend our lives drawing the outline of a house where we can feel at home. When it collapses, we start afresh somewhere else. We always start afresh. Or we die.

I've tried to picture your new place in Brazil. I saw tremendous untidiness. Ashtrays, sheets of paper on the floor covered with mathematical formulas, your navy blue clothes tossed in a heap on a chair. And white silk underwear, the kind you always liked to see me in. For the first time, I could look at that image. What I must do now is tuck it inside a frame, a tiny frame hooked onto my memory. Then it wouldn't be floating around everywhere in my head any more. Everywhere, and nowhere.

3
Chapter Three

In spite of the heat I chose to walk. I could have taken the
bus. Or the subway. Or a cab. I chose to walk with my
manuscript under my arm. As I was leaving I greeted my
neighbour in Spanish, then stepped onto the sidewalk. My
translation had crossed the threshold of the house, the
separation had begun. The street was sweating. Old-age
pensioners were asleep in the shade of their balconies. The
maples were being scorched by the sun. I walked down the
street all the while thinking of the wilderness, forty days and
forty nights — a two-hour walk couldn't possibly be enough.

The handle of my briefcase already felt damp, the
leather was soaking up the stickiness of my hand. I would

114   soon be setting this down in front of the publisher. Every
exertion, every heartbeat, was bringing me closer to that
small death. Two years, almost two years of work about to
come to an end in a downtown office. This was my body,
this was my blood — all the pitfalls of the original text, the
subterfuges and tricks I had needed to come up with in order
to preserve the music of the text at the risk of sacrificing its
meaning. Those long evenings spent chanting the syllables
to myself while you calculated surface dimensions in your
study. Those wonderful bursts of elation when unexpectedly
the resonance of a phrase fastened onto a distinct image, and
the many, many disappointments, when I was unable to give
the words new life in my own language.

Where was I? The sun was so hot now the trees no
longer trembled, and still I walked, I would plod on until I
reached that office on the sixth floor of a building only a few
streets away from the one where you worked for twelve
years. Soon I would be passing by our apartment, it was the
apartment where I had done most of my translation after all,
not just where we had kissed each other for the last time.

The manuscript had withstood your leaving. In my
briefcase I was carrying proof of my survival. I had learnt to
walk again, proudly — to plunge into the noises of the city,
dodge the traffic, translate the voice of another woman. Yet I
wasn't only carrying *her* voice through the din but my own as
well, my survivor's voice.

Our apartment. I stopped across the avenue at the bus
stop. No curtains on the patio door, no activity inside. Then
a huge black cat came and pressed its nose against the
screen, a hideous cat, and all my muscles relaxed. It was
another place now, we didn't live there any more.

An ambulance drove past. Then a bus. And a truck. And
another truck. I had forgotten about the racket from the
traffic in summer, about the ribbon of black dust along the
window ledges, about the sun relentlessly beating down on
my desk on July afternoons, about your testiness when our
neighbour turned on her radio at seven in the morning. You
would withdraw into a stony silence, you wouldn't kiss me

goodbye. I'd forgotten your mood swings, your occasional fits of rage, you were only human and I'd forgotten.

Behind the patio door I could now make out a shadow. A grey-haired woman pushed the screen door open and the big cat stepped out onto the balcony. He was monstrously black. Revolting. He walked up to the wrought-iron railing as if he were looking for me. I gripped the handle of my briefcase. All my memories were turning black, I started to run.

I fled. I fervently hoped that you would never come back. That you would never see what I just saw. Because if you did, I'm sure you would lose any little bit of love you still have for me.

4
Chapter Four

"Life is an endless search for a pair of eyes in which our gaze might lose itself forever." I copied this phrase into my red notebook. I don't know who will say it. Anybody, I suppose. It is a universal assertion, it comes from a false memory, the kind of memory that desperately tries to touch up the past.

François is still asleep. He arrived without letting me know. The doorbell rang twice — another student trying to sell me chocolate, I thought, but I found myself staring at my brother who was exhausted and had a long beard. He had come by bus from New York.

My little brother. We hugged each other, more because it was the conventional thing to do, than out of love. We felt intimidated, we would have to relearn gestures of affection. Vincent joined us, I introduced them to each other. François went pale, Mama hadn't told him that you had left. A quick handshake and, after that, nothing. Silence. Then Vincent came up with an appointment as a pretext and excused himself, he would call me in the evening.

Now we were alone, face to face, we had no choice but to confront our uneasiness. I started off with his trip, life in the United States, my own life, our break-up. The word slipped out. Until then it used to be caught on my tongue, it wouldn't cross the barrier of my lips. "Break-up." I said it again as though I were taking a pair of scissors and cutting a wedding photograph in half. I kept saying it, perhaps I was trying to get François's approval. At first he didn't react, then, with a frown, he admitted, "I never liked Jérôme." That was all, just that true confession splashing cold light on the carpet. I knew he wasn't going to elaborate, at least not now.

I got up to go and cook the pasta. Meanwhile he could settle in upstairs, hang up his clothes, take a bath, lie down. Were these the words of a sister or a mother, I briefly wondered, but this thought was quickly pushed away by a series of everyday acts — washing the vegetables, boiling water, chopping parsley — acts that take our minds off difficult insights.

Neither Bénédicte nor François liked you. How about Philippe? And Anne? Or Mama? My landscape had just changed totally again, I was discovering huge piles of stones on the green lawns, debris, and dead birds.

I waited until my anxiety dissolved, like an acrid flavour or medicine on the tongue. I uncorked a bottle of Chianti. It was fruity, light in the mouth, almost mellow. François had come back down in his dressing-gown and although he didn't used to drink he poured himself a glass of wine. It was something I had never seen him do.

Such a strange evening. I ate opposite a man who in a deliberate way would lift a wineglass to his lips and set it down on the pink tablecloth with a tiny thump. Then the woman next door began to sing. Her voice rose up even

118   before the sun had set, she seemed to be singing for François, only for him. She had taken him away from me from the very first notes, she enveloped him, lulled him.

All evening long I was hoping for something to happen that could be stored in my real memory. But I was sure nothing would.

Chapter Five

In just a few minutes the light slipped away and the sky became wet. People ran in all directions. They were looking for shelter, taking refuge in the cafeteria, heading for their cars. I was the only one left on my bench, except for an old man who sat gazing at the tiny steely spikes jabbing the surface of the pond. The rain clung to my eyelashes, trickled down my neck. My blouse stuck to my skin. But it never occurred to me to get up. It was as though the space around me was completely clogged up.

"I never liked Jérôme." Only this phrase hammering in my head. Oddly enough, it hadn't come back to me when I first woke up. I was probably too preoccupied with that

120   stranger sleeping in my brand-new sofa bed. He would get
        up soon, shave, sit down across from me, and the gulf would
        widen even more. We wouldn't be able to gather around a
        long-ago childhood in an old red-brick house. A modest
        family — a mother whose eyes were dull with resignation, a
        father who hadn't learned how to comfort us. A sister who,
        without knowing it, was preparing for her abduction.

        I put some pink blusher on my cheeks and went out. I
        didn't even ask myself where my steps might take me.
        Everything was becoming mixed-up in my mind, streets,
        trees, cafés, habits. And so I found myself in the park, near
        the pond, only to overhear this confession, "I never loved
        him." A young woman was confiding in a female friend while
        her son threw bits of bread to a duck.

        I thought of the unresponsive look in Mama's eyes when
        you told her about your trips. François's inscrutable smile on
        those rare occasions when he met you, Bénédicte's sulky
        pout. But I was hopeful. I was sure you would eventually win
        them over, Bénédicte as well as the others — they would be
        charmed by you. But the same sulky pout appeared without
        fail on Bénédicte's lips, Mama's fixed smile returned, François
        would mechanically nod his head like a doctor. The miracle
        hadn't happened and yet the earth kept turning, soft and
        round — it at least hadn't let us down.

        "I just can't understand," Bénédicte had said one night
        when we were sharing secrets with each other. I wasn't
        asking anyone to understand. Can we ever find the words to
        explain attraction, hands moving down our body, roughly
        cut fingernails, or a clumsy phrase? Do we only love men
        who are exactly like us? I had cried out and my voice echoed
        deep into the countryside, beyond the rippling lake, to
        where darkness gathered at the foot of the mountain, and
        the horizon burst into flame. I had got up. Furious, I stared
        out at the immensity of the world.

        But you loved me too. I could always find things to say
        in your defence. Now, nothing would come to me.

Chapter Six

François was slowly drinking his beer. Every once in a while he stretched his head toward the sheet of rain behind the window, he appeared lost in thought, but then he would remember that I existed and give me a pensive look. Seldom had twilight seemed so close to evening to me, evening so close to the night, the night so close to an uncomplicated understanding of things.

Sitting on the sofa, my legs tucked under me, I was drinking a hot toddy in tiny gulps while drying my hair. I had come home so totally drenched that both of us burst out laughing. A trace of our childhood had surfaced between us — François mimicked Mama, when she told

122 Philippe and him off. "Why did you play in the rain? You're going to get the flu again." She saw what we didn't see — long nights of coughing, not being able to sleep, being tired. Being worried.

Mama's voice. Mama's scolding. That was all, yet suddenly we were the same flesh and blood again. We had grown inside the same body. One fine morning we had been laid down in the same white wooden cradle. No matter how long we were separated, that memory would never be erased.

François's eyes kept going from the rain to my hair, then from my hair to his glass, and I let that circular motion envelop me. I was calm now. I had faith in the memory of the generations. François did too, I think, or he wouldn't have been so trusting, I wouldn't have clearly heard, "I've stopped looking for Noëlle. I've come back for good."

None of us, neither Mama, Philippe nor I, had ever linked François's going away to Noëlle's disappearance. I brought my hand to my cheek as though he had slapped my face. Too much distance fell away all at once. I felt dizzy— it was the same heartbreak, the same expression on his face and mine, both of us waiting. Dizzy, or feverish perhaps, my cheeks burned. I was confronted with a problem of distance. Yes, that's what it was. We were runaway planets in an erratic sky, we were spinning madly around each other, we might at any moment smash into one another.

I wanted François to tell me exactly in what cities he had hoped to find her. A whole string of names filed by: Edmonton, Vancouver, Seattle, San Francisco, Las Vegas, Miami, Chicago, New York. Why those cities and not others? "Why not?" he said, Noëlle could be living anywhere, she was intangible, as immaterial as a ghost in a mirror. François had given up. He didn't look like a hero any more, he was coming back shouldering his defeat.

Only soft drops were falling from the clouds now, they slid down the windowpane. François smiled at me. I noticed a line running from each corner of his lips to his nose, the first wrinkle, imperceptible almost, but already there. For good, I thought. The air wasn't quite as muggy any more, a breeze gently stirred the curtain, it was becoming easier to breathe. Ensconced in your leather armchair, my little brother was sipping his beer with a tender look in his eyes. So then, without thinking, I crossed the two metres of patterned carpet between us and snuggled down in his arms, unafraid, confident, the way we approach someone who has stepped through the looking-glass. Someone who would never destroy us.

7

Chapter Seven

It wasn't a postcard, which I would have tacked next to the others on the notice-board in the kitchen. No, a letter, a long letter in a small, fine hand that took some deciphering. It was writing revealing surprise and emotion, in which I sensed the haunting light of Crete mixed with sorrow, too much clarity and softness, too many sources of light intersecting without merging with one another in the immaculate blueness.

Madame Girard doesn't want to come home. One would never have thought that she lived in my house for forty years without travelling. "I'm staying," she wrote, "I'm continuing my search." She was at a hotel by the sea in

Heracleion. Every morning she took a bus to Knossos, it was a pilgrimage. She would walk among the ruins, picture life in that great labyrinth, think of the legend of the Minotaur, and Ariadne, Ariadne and her clew.

I read and reread that vibrant script on the thin sheets of paper in anxious wonderment. Then, as though it were a love letter, I hid the envelope away in a book. I wasn't going to mention it to Vincent. At least not right away. This letter was too close to me.

To François I made the excuse that I had some urgent errands to run and I went out. The house was too cramped, I was going to wander all through the city from east to west, along the great thoroughfares, into the churches and the cemetery, up the mountain. I was going to be as dazzled as Madame Girard. A discreet but determined sun immersed the landscape in light, and the farther away I got, the more it seemed to me that the world was only there for us to travel resolutely through while we left our troubles behind.

From the top of the mountain I gazed down at the city and I began to drift along the river, to the gulf, to the sea, all the way to the obscure force that is needed to start over again. I felt the dramatic swaying of life, outside of boundaries and frontiers, beyond the prison of the past. Then, I saw you, in Brazil. I also saw Monsieur Girard's blood in the basement's dust, and Noëlle, the three of you in one and the same vision which faded behind the mysterious eternity of time. I saw myself, serene and detached.

One day you and I would see each other again, one day we would pass by one another in a strange land and you would simply have become an abstraction from days gone by, a man like any other man. We would greet each other without bitterness, "Hello, how are you?" Just that impersonal phrase which former lovers say when the longing has disappeared.

I saw myself as detached. This is how I saw myself, with flowing roots in the brightness of a day that had swallowed time.

At home François was sitting in the leather armchair

126   waiting for me. Across from him, Vincent. They were chatting about foreign countries, the States, Italy. I poured myself something to drink and sat down cross-legged on the sofa. They thought I looked wistful, where had I been then? All day I had followed a thread that took me a long, long way from here. Right up to a door opening out onto both sides of time. But I wouldn't have known how to tell them this.

Chapter Eight

We were all assembled in the dining-room. Mama,
Philippe, Anne, the children, François. And, for the first
time, Vincent.

It was a real Sunday. Mama wore a silky dress. François,
her little François, was coming back to her. She had trouble
believing it, we were all going to be together from now on.
It seemed as if she didn't miss Noëlle. For a couple of days
she would come out of her pining for the past, but then the
void would assert itself again, like silence before people say
goodbye. And we would have to try to make her feel better.
I would ask her out to the movies or rent a Hollywood film
which would bring back memories of earlier days, with

128   women wearing old-fashioned make-up. For a couple of minutes I would succeed.

Well, actually, I would fail. She'd brighten as she remembered those names she used to know so well, then her eyelids would drop down a little, she would retreat to a solitary place deep inside herself. I would plead guilty once again, I hadn't been able to save her.

On the table I had laid out salads, cold meats, hors d'oeuvres, paper napkins with extravagant prints, and pink carnations. I had thought of everything. The day before, I'd gone shopping at the Italian market with Vincent and François. The three of us strolled for a long time among fragrances and colours, our arms loaded up with groceries. We were excited, the party had already begun. We picked out the fruit piece by piece, tasted the sausages, bought so many spices it was as if we'd just discovered the route to the Indies. These were moments of abundance, tenderness, and dreams all wrapped up together. The day had slipped away from the continuity of time. Also, I liked the subtle rapport between Vincent and François, it seemed to stem from having renounced something. I saw in their attitudes the easing of a heartache that had now been accepted. Their sorrow no longer tormented them, they were ready for joy.

At noon, though, it was a different François. He walked over to Mama to kiss her, folded her gingerly into his arms as if he were afraid he might crush her by hugging her too tightly. After that, he sat down beside her and fell silent. He was the baby again, the one who lets himself be treated and loved as a child, even though he's already a man. As we clinked glasses to toast his plans I saw a shadow come into his eyes, the regret that he had grown up.

But in the maple tree on the lawn a squirrel appeared with a nut in his mouth, and Pascal started to shout, stretching out his little fingers toward it. Mama got up to take him in her arms — *he* was the baby now. They went up to the window and the shadow vanished from François's eyes. His voice returned, his grown-up voice, as he joined in the conversation Vincent, Anne, Philippe and I were having.

Mama stepped outside with Pascal and Véronique, their hands full of peanuts, but we carried on talking, putting all our verbs in the future tense.

That familiar lump wasn't there. I didn't notice it at the time, only after they left. François is the one who, without knowing what my question was, has come up with the answer. In the clear light of midday we had managed to fix happy images in our minds.

9
Chapter Nine

I said, "Human existence is a screenplay with the same scenes repeating themselves over and over." Falling in love, trying to hold on to that love, seeing it crumble, losing it. Only the character's face changes. Another fold under the chin, a few more grey hairs.

Bénédicte is at the very beginning, her world has just lit up. Vincent and I have reached phase two, we are creating reference points. Vincent is already talking about our next vacation and I'm not even startled. I go along with his fantasy. This isn't really a lie, but rather an implicit faith in life. At first it struck me as being a naïve sort of faith, but I've changed my opinion, it feels more like hope.

I don't know why I shared my thoughts with François. He listened carefully even though he wasn't quite sure what I meant. So far, François has only had brief affairs, the kind of involvement where a break-up doesn't seem like a loss. Then he quipped that some day he would like a love affair that lasted. Desire wasn't enough for him any more. He spoke with the same determination in his voice as Vincent. He glanced through the job ads in the paper. The day before, he had been at the employment office. Today he was planning to meet with the managers of the major hotels. He was sure to find something eventually, even if it was outside of his line of work — hadn't he always managed in the past?

Did I ever tell him? The scene was still terribly fresh in my mind. I had stopped by the house; Papa had been hurt on the job and needed to rest for a few days so we were trying to entertain him. Mama was just taking a cake out of the oven when the doorbell rang, it was registered mail. Papa put his glasses on and awkwardly signed the piece of paper the postal employee held out to him. Then he took the mailing-tube which was addressed to him. It contained an electrician's diploma with François's name printed on it in a beautiful script and with a red seal. Rolled inside the certificate was a hastily scribbled note, "Keep this for me," followed by the initial "F," that was all. François had taken courses in Vancouver without any of us knowing.

Papa just stood there, speechlessly, holding the parchment. Suddenly he left the house without saying where he was going. He came back with a gilt frame and a bottle of vermouth, I would help him find the best spot to hang the diploma and after that stay for dinner. Mama winked happily at me. Papa was ecstatic. He had forgotten about *my* diplomas as well as Philippe's.

Even so, I kept smiling. Mama put an Edith Piaf record on the turntable, poured us all generous portions of vermouth and sat down with me to smoke a cigarette. With a girlish playfulness she blew smoke rings into the air, then started to talk about Grandmama in words I'd never heard her use before, words we say when we can begin to cherish a

132   mother from whom we no longer expect patience or love. I
listened to her and didn't dare move in the old creaky chair.
Mama was talking to me as a mother talks to her daughter
while Papa was rediscovering his son.

Some day I would talk to her too, I would ask her what
had been lost between us. Perhaps some day there would be
a free space on the right side of her heart.

She did inquire though, "And how about you?" I took
the easy way, I chatted about you. We had just moved in
together, I was euphoric. I spent my evenings decorating the
apartment as if the future of the planet depended on it — I
wanted warm colours, to protect us. I hadn't been bold
enough to talk about myself.

Phase two, that's where we were, Vincent and I, at that
point when one doesn't wish to know that the end already
lurks inside the beginning. Unless it's the love between a
daughter and her mother. Then we store up our passionate
feelings in a vast memory bank. Then there is no beginning
and no end, only a meandering journey on which the truth
never gets totally lost.

10

Chapter Ten

I opened my engagement book to check an appointment and this is what caught my eye — the name "Étienne," in capital letters. Just under the figure seven. Your son's birthday. Today. I closed my engagement book again without noticing that my appointment was written down under the figure eight. A little voice urged me to phone him. Another little voice whispered, is that really necessary?

I didn't think for a moment that *you* would phone him. Your son was waiting for some sign from you — you knew that, yet you wouldn't respond. It would be a day like any other day for you. You would eat, you would work, perhaps you would make love without giving a single thought to his unhappiness.

134   Outside, a tall and lanky man was pushing a tiny little girl on a candy-floss pink bicycle. All of a sudden that image became unbearable.

I twice dialled the wrong number. I had to hang up and take a deep breath. With a bit of luck there would be no answer, I would leave a message, and if Étienne wasn't angry with me any more, he'd call me back.

Nobody there. I listened to Judith's message to the end, then expressed my best wishes in that shaky voice I get when my heart cowers against my ribs. At least I had done the right thing.

On the sidewalk the little girl had ridden her bicycle back and forth a few times without toppling over. The man clapped. This time I looked closely at the tall, lanky man and the tiny girl. And suddenly a blind rage engulfed me. It came out of nowhere, like a tidal wave surging over the beach and then over the city, the country, the whole world, covering trees and crosses, houses and schools, sweeping away barns and animals, wrecking, devastating, destroying, drowning, killing, killing, killing everything in savage carnage. It came out of nowhere, a black hole in my brain, in my heart, in my bones, an unimaginable abyss in which your blue and bloated corpse appeared on top of the waves.

When my own way of seeing returned, I looked at the world differently. I could now see through things, even the bugs dangling from the thread of my thoughts.

11

Chapter Eleven

Noëlle would always be a teenager. He would always picture her in her short skirts and with too much eye-shadow, even when he was an old man, so tired he would have forgotten the cutmarks his skates used to leave on the ice in winter, and furtive embraces under the lilacs. What else did François remember? Details so flimsy they had no real substance, insignificant fragments fused together to form a portrait of Noëlle that he couldn't share with anyone.

I let it drop. I didn't allude again to the look of wonder that had illuminated her face when she'd felt the small warm body of her brother in her arms for the first time, or to the blue scarf she had knitted for him. I didn't mention, as Mama

136 always made a point of saying, she had spoiled him, completely spoiled him.

Then suddenly this had stopped. She had closed her bedroom door behind her without letting him come in, she wanted to be alone with her dreams, she would dream all day long. What on earth could she be thinking about? Papa would ask, but *I* knew — I used to hear her whispering in her sleep, "Mi amor, mi amor." Well before her handsome stranger came along.

One afternoon I had found François asleep in front of the closed door, his eyelashes wet with tears. That was the end of it, amnesia had set in. He had gone back to playing with Philippe, he would eat again and laugh again.

I let it drop. Of his own accord he started to talk once more about Noëlle. He thought he had spotted her in New York on a wide avenue. She was brown-haired and graceful, but large dark circles under her eyes stood out against her cheeks. He had begun to shake. That woman, who looked so tired for a thirty-seven-year-old, was not Noëlle. Without making any gesture, he had let her go by him.

Every night after work he had returned to that same avenue. Every day for months he wandered through the jam-packed crowds where faces superimposed themselves endlessly on other faces until they all blended into one hazy, transparent image. Until he became frantic and desperate, until he almost went mad. This is when he decided to come back.

I haven't done any work today, haven't written a thing, not a single line of dialogue. I didn't even jot down any ideas for the script. I carried my red notebook from the desk to the kitchen table, then from the kitchen to the living-room, along with the image of a brown-haired, graceful woman who at thirty-seven already had such dark shadows under her eyes. It was an apparition, a ghostly coming together of childhood and old age, short skirts and death.

And as if that weren't enough, all afternoon the road just in front of the house was being dug up. I would have to put up with the stupefying noise from the pneumatic drills. I hid out in my bedroom, I had given up, not a sentence of my script was going to get written. I curled up and fell asleep.

The sound of voices woke me up. The street had become quiet. In the kitchen, Vincent and François were cooking dinner while I slowly emerged from a dream about a strange brown-haired man with dark circles under his eyes who was hurrying along between huge buildings on a wide avenue in New York. That was you. I had let you pass by me without doing anything to stop you. And I felt no remorse.

Chapter Twelve

The darkness no longer clings as tightly to the night, but it hasn't yet vanished, it lingers like grief. I wrote "grief" without thinking. It came the way images come, from a flaw in the mind, from a dropped stitch in a piece of knitting that otherwise would have been too perfect. In my notebook, life is disintegrating and I watch it disintegrate without being afraid. I feel a kind of serenity in the word "grief," all I need do is make it rhyme with "leaf" to imagine a budding happiness underneath its skin.

As I opened my eyes a short while ago I saw words, thousands of words strung together in the dark. I quietly got up, picked up my notebook from the chest of drawers,

listened to Vincent's regular breathing and closed the door
behind me. It's a slight, peaceful spell of insomnia. I
scribbled several pages while I thought about François, his
waiting for Noëlle, his looking for her every day, his
hopeless search gradually wearing him out and how he had
finally broken down, become frantic, almost gone mad.
There were no more stars at night where he had gone.

Perhaps in his sleep he passes through a hell without
flames, a hell so icy it shatters the bones. Or a garden with
gigantic plants, like the ones in the high-rise building he will
be managing.

They phoned him yesterday evening after we'd had our
dessert. He let out a whoop, then whirled me around in his
arms just like Papa did when he got his promotion. Without
telling anyone we were coming, we went to pick up Mama
and, after that, turned up at Anne and Philippe's. We drank
summer drinks as we stretched the evening out until we were
so tired we could barely keep our eyes open. Even Mama.
Even the children, because none of us had been able to make
them go to sleep. An almost visible vibration was in the air
— our muscles relaxed, we let our guard down, for once we
weren't expecting or receiving painful news. I rested my
head on Vincent's shoulder and didn't think any more about
Mama's wrinkles or love affairs that would fall apart. I was
oblivious to all that, I was learning how to forget.

Anne's stomach resembles a large egg. It will be a girl,
she already knows this. "Why not call her Noëlle?" Mama
suggested. But we all shook our heads at the same time. Not
Noëlle, better a name that belongs to the present.

In my notebook a tiny girl slowly unfolds next to Anne's
heartbeat, François's face has lit up now, Madame Girard is
burying her sorrow in the splendour of ruins, daybreak is near.
I am writing. Vincent is asleep, so is François, and Philippe. I
don't need to protect them. I feel as though I were betraying
my language and, within my language, Mama's unhappiness,
and the shadowy eyes of a woman I find it impossible to
picture as my sister. I am betraying myself as well. I am
writing in a language that I do not remember.

Chapter Thirteen

He rang the doorbell, three short rings as we'd agreed, and he walked in, shouting, "It's me!" the way he used to when Judith would drop him off for the weekend. Taken aback, Vincent carefully inspected this hippie who doesn't quite look like a man yet. I introduced them to each other, Étienne, Vincent, and left it at that. I waited for the questions but they didn't come. He wanted to see the house, every nook and cranny. He lingered for a long time in the room where your things are piled up, he sat down in your swivel chair with a far-away look in his eyes and asked me where his bed was. I pointed at the mattress against the wall, behind some boxes. Then I had the presence of mind to drag him off to my study, he would now sleep on the brand-new sofa bed. He felt the cushions with his hand which was still chubby. He looked at me with a smile. I had passed the test.

Maybe *you* were going to arrive at any moment too. You would ring the doorbell, three short rings, and you'd walk in as you always did at night. A sob was caught in my throat. I seemed to be travelling up a river, all the way to its streams which came cascading down from the mountain, then up the streams to their sources, some of which were underground. The river, the streams, and the sources. Ten years.

"Are you sad?" I didn't deny it. We sat down on the sofa bed and I talked to him the way people talk when they don't care any more what impression they make. In short bursts which shattered the quietness of the room. I spoke of the heart going numb and us not understanding why, of bodies hanging in the middle of a bedroom, of utter despair gripping us and how much strength it takes to resist, of time turning in on itself, more and more, and then one day time beating normally again, carrying the heart along with it, time that we now measure in hours and days and nights — we don't know how this happens but it isn't by chance. Then I stopped. He looked up and said simply, "You don't talk like a mother."

Vincent came to get us. He had made a huge salad, would we do him the honour of joining him? Étienne accepted, yes, he would stay. Afterwards we would go and help François paint. He had found an apartment downtown and hoped to move in as quickly as possible. Étienne wanted to come along, he loved to paint, all we had to do was let Judith know.

He wolfed down his salad, the way teenagers do, while watching Vincent out of the corner of his eye.

I was watching too, feeling a bit shaken. At my table your son was winning over my new love with descriptions of his summer camp. And Vincent was listening with amusement. When the conversation flagged, he would even restart it. I was observing them as I used to observe

142   Grandmama making quilts, those hundreds of squares she patiently sewed together with her elderly fingers, the scraps of her life. She would tell the story of times past, over there Mama's dress, over here Uncle Jean's coat. I never tired of watching her work. I was already learning to turn a lot of discarded pieces into a single life.

14

Chapter Fourteen

"I love you, Emma." These were the first words I heard this morning. I felt a kiss on my forehead and Vincent left. He quietly went down the stairs and the front door squeaked a little bit. Through half-opened eyes I saw that the bedroom was in a mess, wineglasses and scattered clothes littering the chest of drawers.

I thought to myself, a room can be untidy in such a way that it attracts words of love, it forms crinkles of joy around our eyes. The world no longer looks like a wasteland. Then I said to myself, I'm going to be forty. But I simply couldn't make the connection between my age, love, and the bedroom's untidiness. Just as well, since good

144   luck or bad luck so often comes between cause and effect. I
only noted that I see things on an ever-smaller scale. As if
it could all fit into my hand, terms of endearment, happy
plans and heartaches.

When Vincent says, "I love you, Emma," he pulls me to
the right side of the world. My name suggests a broken
heart that will never mend, it is as sad as a clock that has
stopped. Papa's mother was called Emma. She died before I
could get to know her. Mama lay in her hospital bed, she
held me in her arms, Papa didn't dare come near me yet.
What were they going to call her? Emma, like your mother,
Mama proposed. Papa must have agreed; yes, Emma, I was
joining his family.

Then later, much later, there was that other story when
I came home from school one evening. I had put *Madame
Bovary* on the table and Mama's face had lit up. She pressed
the book to her heart. Such a great novel! Such a wonderful
woman, that Emma Rouault! She had died for love. Papa
was puzzled. He asked us to tell him what it was about.
When we did, he picked the book up, he who could barely
read, and said that it was beyond him. How could one end
up like that, the woman was some kind of lunatic, wasn't
she? Mama's cheeks turned purple, we couldn't believe how
angry she got, she flew into a great rage — Papa didn't
understand, he hadn't understood anything right from the
beginning, he never had. Sobbing, she went to her
bedroom and locked herself in.

I can still see us around the table. Papa with his head in
his hands, Noëlle lifting the book up with her fingertips,
François huddles against Noëlle while Philippe's eyes search
out Papa's. I'm not looking at anyone. I'm not there. Before
even having loved, I have already died twice.

15

Chapter Fifteen

A small patch in the maple tree has turned yellow, one tiny splash of yellow in a sea of green, and oddly enough the green seems almost completely uniform, as though it were offering resistance. The summer is holding its own, but that small yellow patch is sweeping across my window, it is trying to find a foothold in reality.

Last year you said, while looking out at the first yellow leaves, "The world is unfolding as it should," and you went back to your equations. But *I* saw a long string of disasters, another assassination attempt, yet another war, that woman who had been stabbed in a public square, and a new guardedness whenever I came near you. The world never

146 turns like a well-oiled machine. Today, though, it's making an exception, it's breathing peacefully, it doesn't threaten us.

That could be because of my script. I've spread the pages out on my desk, all the scenes, each with its share of inconsistencies, lines that don't fit the characters' voices or that sum up a situation too quickly, and also the ones that ring true. Surprisingly, those always end up in Madame Girard's mouth. That is what I call her for now, Madame Girard. I just can't give her a name that separates her from real life. As though I wanted to see her, touch her and hear her, as though her name, when tacked onto me, could animate the words.

Last night we settled down in bed with the window wide open so we could hear the neighbour's singing, and I read out a few scenes to Vincent. He commented on the tone, the plot, the characters. He didn't see Madame Girard the same way I do. For a little while I felt alone with my imaginings. But we talked it over and the feeling grew fainter. We disagreed, yet that didn't matter, because together we were poring over words that were being given a soul in the fading light of day. It was one of those unforgettable moments when something new begins between lovers, a shared enthusiasm in which the act of invention plays a part. For the first time I thought of my script as a project belonging to both of us.

The air is so soft today. François called, he is enjoying his apartment and wanted my advice about furniture. He's decorating, making a life for himself in which small things have become important. He, too, is trying to make his dreams come true. He is observant. I would never have believed that one day I would get my brother back.

I would never have believed either that I would get Étienne back. He stopped by this afternoon with a friend, they were out cycling. He introduced us and went over to the refrigerator for some juice without asking me if it was all right. I smiled happily, he felt at home here again. He then showed his friend around the house, all the rooms except the one where your things are stored. He has shut off that memory when you and I were together. I now exist in the present.

The same goes for Judith. I received a card from her on which was written in her small handwriting, "Thank you about Étienne. He needs it so badly." Just these words and her signature.

I thought, it isn't true everything vanishes as in that chanson by Léo Ferré. Some grief will ease as time goes by, some ruins can receive light, some stories have an unexpected ending. It isn't as though we forget, a patch of yellow still sweeps across the window, but we don't see the coming of autumn as we used to.

16
Chapter Sixteen

I just couldn't read his expression. That stranger wasn't Vincent. A tragic face but with a peculiar fire glowing deep in his eyes, a kind of anxious rapture. I sat down by the window in a ray of already slanting sunlight so a bit of warmth would touch my shoulders.

I didn't have to wait. He spoke right away. To the point. Elena was in Toronto for a film. She was asking him to join her there, they had had this passion for each other after all.

I thought about your going away. I thought about Madame Girard, about history repeating itself, about my life as a tiny civilisation stuck in a circular path. He was leaving very early the next morning. He said, "It would be better if I slept at my own place tonight." I agreed. I needed to be alone too.

With you I would have cooked dinner as if nothing had happened, we would have spent the evening together, we would have slept in the same bed. So the cycle really was being broken somewhat.

"I hope you aren't blaming me," is what he said in the hall just before he left. I shook my head. I was blaming myself. I never *would* be strong enough to stop people from leaving. I didn't cry when he hugged me. I even blew him a kiss and went back to search out that ray of sunshine, it now fell on my legs. There was a cool breeze coming in. I closed the window.

I let my eyes wander all over the room, then I tried to focus on the details, on bits of décor one never looks at, the rectangle between the carpet and the wall, the angle of the ceiling in the farthest corner, the tiny crack that would grow longer a few years from now — that was damage one could anticipate. And repair.

I dreamed of a love affair that would be like a house. Next year I was going to put flowers in boxes on the edge of the balcony. Maybe I would plant a garden, why not, with vegetables and herbs along the fence, chives and fresh basil for pasta.

I wasn't hungry just then. I decided to go out. To walk in the streets among people I would never know, to keep on going through the park, stopping briefly by the pond. To walk to Madame Girard's apartment, choose a book from her bookcase that might have an explanation for disasters more terrible than mine, the lions of the Coliseum, the Trojan War, the tidal wave that had caused Knossos to be abandoned.

I spent my evening reading gilt-edged books. I didn't spend it deep inside my bed rolled up in a ball as I did last November.

I went home. One by one, the stars lit up. The air was fragrant. It was one of those evenings when fear isn't really able to seep into our pores. Vincent was going to join Elena,

150   probably he was still in love with her. And yet between him and me I sensed there was already an attachment as resilient as a memory. I sensed it. During lovemaking bodies don't lie.

Then I pictured Elena's graceful figure and I felt uncertain. I saw your face. Were we perhaps condemned to forever push the same stone up a mountain without succeeding in rolling it all the way to the top? I felt uncertain. But not completely. Vincent had left a message on the answering machine. "See you soon, Emma." In the silence of the house I murmured, "See you soon, Vincent." As if it were a magic formula that could ward off fate.

17

Chapter Seventeen

We smiled at each other. Not out of politeness, it was a real smile, open and free — she didn't just want to be my girlfriend's lover to me. As she went over to the sound system she asked me what I would like to hear. I crouched down beside her and we took the discs out of the stand. For quite a while she compared the various recordings, then asked me to choose one. I chose a Bach concerto and the music rose up in the room. I closed my eyes as if I were praying to a faceless god having neither doctrine nor divine benevolence and who only existed for a few seconds. I forgot about June and June forgot about me.

We didn't hear Bénédicte come in. Suddenly she stood

152   before us, her arms loaded up with bags. She was sorry, she had been caught in a traffic jam. Then she stopped. She had only just *really* seen us, as we sat there on the floor, reverently listening among all the discs. She burst out laughing. So did June. I did too. Who could have anticipated that aperitif-time would have a late-night look about it? Bénédicte was thrilled. Her normal tone of voice had returned, her gestures cut up space into measurable parts.

June was here to stay, I felt that right away. She wasn't a fleeting presence — her face showed an eagerness to make things last, to say no to loneliness. Perhaps her serenity had something to do with music, with the sheets of paper she filled up with notes, or with the specks of light illuminating her skin, or with longing, the longing for an island where she would never live again. June had the self-assurance of people who know they cannot take anything for granted.

Later, when we were having our dessert, I noticed that Bénédicte had stopped counting. The number of interviews she would have to do this year, vacation days, promotions. She was gently floating along on a raft, she was drifting toward an indistinct point on the horizon where numbers no longer had any hold on time.

This past night I was drowning. Bénédicte glided by me on a raft of feathers without seeing me. But June blew forcibly into her flute and Bénédicte came back toward me, just as I was going to slip below the waves. I woke up with that image, my hand, already blue, in Bénédicte's warm hand. And June who was watching us from her island through the reflections of the sun on her instrument.

I wanted to fling myself into Vincent's arms, but the place beside me was empty. He was probably asleep in Elena's bed at that very moment. I sat up and turned on the night light to try and clear all the water from my chest. Bit by bit the dream receded until only the last image remained — us joining hands while the melody rang out more and more clearly in the bedroom. And I saw June. With her quiet yet powerful music she was linking causes to their effects.

18

Chapter Eighteen

Time does not flow continuously in Mama's life. She has cut up the years into irregular strips, then put these into albums she sometimes opens after supper, as daylight sinks behind the mountain. It is the red one with the Christmas wreaths she looks at first. The photos smell of oranges and Mama looks like a doll in Grandpapa's arms. Nearby, her hands folded over her stomach, Grandmama is expecting another birth. She has a surprised look in her eyes, she is amazed at the mystery of it all. How could these hips of hers transform a simple surge of love into a small pink body?

But Mama doesn't interpret things the way I do. She tells me secretly, "She is hoping for a boy." She says that every

154   time. And every time I try to stifle a silent little scream and I turn the page as if there was no room for me in that enormous stomach. I dream up some ruse to make Mama close that portion of time, to have her open *my* childhood, in the blue album, and hold in her hands those moments when the two of us are alone together. Without Papa or Noëlle. There aren't many, only three or four, but for me all the books ever written are contained in these bits of yellowed paper.

Then we get to the reminiscing. Over here, I'm playing in the sandbox with Noëlle. Over there, I've just started school — two of my teeth are missing. Somewhere along the way, I don't know when, something was broken. And I am like Mama, I neatly section off time periods. I say "before" and "after," I link these words with disappearance and departure, but I know it happened long before. And so the albums pile up in my head. In my new, orderly memory, grief has the fragrance of oranges and my acceptance of things is as solid as a native land.

Tonight Mama brought out a new album, a green one. There is hardly anything in it yet, it's devoted to François's homecoming. The party I gave at my place. François in Mama's living-room on the old wine-coloured sofa underneath his diploma. The celebration at Anne and Philippe's. And also that photo, which Philippe took, where she beams a radiant, interminable smile at François such as I had never seen her give to anyone, not even Papa. As I sat there holding the photo her face slipped away, it dissolved into a look of jubilant happiness that I would never be part of.

I put the tiny rectangle down on the tablecloth in front of me and wrapped my hands around my cup. They were ice-cold and clammy, maybe because of the lump that was rising up in my throat again. I pretended to be listening as Mama talked on but in my mind I went over an old story: the prodigal son returns and they kill the fatted calf. *He* is the child who brings comfort, not the others, not those who stayed at home. The same probably

goes for Elena. Now that Vincent has returned to her, she
has forgotten about her new lover.

Today I have no confidence any more. I'm frightened.
I'm sinking in waters so deep even Bénédicte wouldn't be
able to come and pull me out.

I am too faithful, I think, to be deeply loved.

Chapter Nineteen

I've been writing. A long letter to Madame Girard, but I don't know yet if I'll mail it. I don't like my tone. The sentences are short, chopped-up, they are the sentences of an asthmatic even though I make a point of repeating, "I'm fine, I'm fine." When I reread them, I noticed immediately: the tight lump was right there, in the small curved characters. There was no denying it.

The great calamities of history are no longer enough, they just can't make my own small misfortunes acceptable to me any more. No matter what I tell myself, Vincent and Jérôme are beginning to form a single face in my head, one and the same story. I haven't heard from Vincent and I'm as worn out as Papa's heart.

I folded the letter and put it down in front of me beside the script. The red notebook is lying open — I'm trying to focus my mind outside of my anxiety, it's not easy. A moment ago I simply couldn't, so I read the completed scenes and after that the notes in an effort to get away from my own voice, to take on the characters' voices. In the left-hand margin I scribbled "shift," then crossed that out and wrote above it "eclipse." Still, it isn't quite that yet. The right term would conjure up that unbroken silence within me where words are inaccurate, disappointing, but at the same time protected by an outer shell of flesh and blood.

Now I no longer call my characters Madame Girard or Monsieur Girard, it is not just my voice that is being eclipsed, it is all of reality. The fiction is gaining ground, it is gradually invading me and I let it sweep over me, I'm not fighting against it but hoping for something like redemption.

I thought of a new scene. The woman slumped over her husband's coffin. The woman in tears. And she slowly draws herself up, first her head, and her chest, her whole body, then she places her hands on her husband's body, she leans on that cold corpse and gets up. She gets back on her feet. That is all I can write today. A woman who has collapsed but gets up again. A woman who is ahead of me. Who is braver than I am.

20
Chapter Twenty

I came home with my arms full of groceries as if preparing for a party. I had walked all the way to the market after I put on a pretty, fresh summer dress and eye make-up. This fitted in with my new-found bravery — looking my best, going shopping, cooking special dishes even if I was going to have dinner by myself. Tonight I would be enjoying my quail *à l'orange* in the dining-room.

I didn't see the blink of the answering machine immediately. Only a little later, while putting things away. I pushed the button without giving it a thought, as I do when I don't expect any particular call. Then I set the can of food down on the counter. Vincent was trying to make himself heard over the noise in a public place, he articulated each syllable so that I could understand. He was at the Toronto airport, would leave soon and land in Montreal at five o'clock. He was anxious to see me. Then his voice became intimate and I heard, "I'll be with you in a few hours, my love." I listened to the message at least a dozen times, just for that one sentence.

I tuned the radio to a station that plays sentimental songs and ran a bath, a festive bath with lots of bubbles. I was also going to change the sheets on my bed, I would put the flowers I had bought in the bedroom. I checked to see if there was any port left in the pantry. And I sank back into the bubbles so the wait wouldn't seem quite so long.

I counted. How many minutes before Vincent would get here, how many months since you left, how many days since I met that man on the street whom I mistook for you. The number of times I had thought about the São Paulo woman. How many years I had left to love, the number of chances to be happy, how many break-ups it takes in a lifetime before we learn. Then I stopped. I would have ended getting everything mixed up, I would have seen too far ahead, I would have forgotten how worried I had been each time I heard someone say, "I'm leaving," and I don't want to forget anything. Get better, yes, but not forget anything.

What time was it now? The plane should already be accelerating down the runway, Vincent was probably looking through the window at the life he was leaving behind and the life he would find again in my arms. He definitely didn't know yet at what altitude the split would take place between the past and the future, the plane wouldn't fly high enough, and he would be heading back to me with Elena's smell still clinging to him. It is such a struggle before we finally become detached.

On the radio a singer moaned about a heartache that stung like a burn. I suddenly saw Vincent as a wounded man. I had to get used to that idea — soon a wounded man would be ringing my doorbell.

21

Chapter Twenty-one

I'm not much of a clairvoyant. No matter how often I lay the tarot cards out on the wooden table and try to read every arcanum, the future remains as impenetrable as a forest on a moonless night. All I see are my senseless fears.

When Vincent set his luggage down in the living-room he was exhausted. One could have sworn he had just come back from a long journey. He walked toward me and he said, "Hold me very tight," and I held him very tight. I had the feeling I was turning into a huge, solid woman, one of those stone statues that in ancient times held up temple roofs while staring out at the sea from afar. I never would have pictured myself like that.

I had put on a disc June had recommended to me, and as the music played he started to talk, in a circumspect way, without betraying Elena's privacy. I liked that discretion. The woman with whom he had been madly in love was now almost a stranger to him. "Already," he added wistfully. The only thing left between them was nostalgia. It wasn't the same with Bénédicte, he didn't know why. Perhaps when absolute passion disappears, it doesn't leave any love behind, only passion's ruins.

I shuddered. Would it be like this for you and me? It might. I had an idea. I would install a lock on the door of the room where your things are. It was silly of me, I knew that, but I was going to install it anyway in case the truth one day decided to leap out at me.

Today is as smooth as a freshly repainted room, peaceful and smooth. We know very well that underneath that fresh coat of paint there are finger marks, lingering traces of an old fit of anger, bitter words and despair, yellow rings from a poor light, but none of that shows any more. It is another room now with different walls, holding a love I snuggle up to, my script on the chest of drawers next to a photo of Étienne in his hippie clothes — it is a life as peaceful and smooth as the one conjured up in enchanting fiction.

But I know perfectly well that the walls will become dirty, they'll witness new angry outbursts, more despair. Some day perhaps Vincent will want to leave again and I won't be as brave as I was this time. I'll stretch out on the bed and pretend I am dead, I'll wait for my body to be cast into the waves. But Vincent laughs and I start to laugh along with him. "I am not Jérôme," he reminds me, we mustn't confuse everything, men and events; life doesn't repeat itself as the seasons do.

So I go along with his fantasies. I don't tell him that in my own reality love *always* vanishes, every kind of love, even the love in friendship, even the love of a brother who doesn't come to see me quite so often any more. I must understand, his work, the apartment, and now that pretty blond new lover, Fabienne, who emerged from a parallel

162 universe as though she had been waiting for him since the beginning of time. My life is like a chapel — people stop to say a prayer there, and when they have found comfort they leave, they are on their way.

But Vincent's hands are tightly holding on to my hips and my confidence comes back. It's because of something he says at the very moment his pleasure mingles with mine, "Look at me." As if deep in my eyes he found a temple of stone to which people return to spend the rest of their lives, while I am staring out at the sea from afar. The sea which isn't as cruel as we think.

Fourth Song

City of Angels

Chapter One

"It's going to rain tonight, the fishing will be good."
Vincent got out the tackle and Étienne clapped his hands
which are already quite big. He cheers at everything
Vincent suggests. He declared in June's language, "I love
fish," and June laughingly corrected him, "Not fish,
fishing." The rowboat forms a tiny patch on the grey water
at the foot of the mountain. From here we can make out
two motionless fluorescent dots above that wider patch. I
insisted Étienne wear a life jacket, and Vincent put his on
while giving me a wink.

A luminous haze is settling over the lake. It blends with
the rich tones of the melody that envelops us. June is

166   preparing for a concert. She has been practising for hours today, playing the same sonata over and over, and this has set off a melancholy mood in me that reaches down so deep it seems as though within my mended spirit there still lingered a vulnerable soul.

The patch in the distance is getting bigger, coming closer. It will soon bring back familiar faces and gestures. Étienne will triumphantly hold up his catch. Vincent will watch him with a smile, as you used to do and I'll make enthusiastic comments as I've done a hundred times before and the three of us will clean the fish so we can eat it tomorrow. Night is falling. In the gathering darkness it will be even easier to confuse you for a little while with Vincent. Then I'll suddenly pull myself together, I'll see the difference between your walk and Vincent's brisker walk. I'll focus on specific gestures of yours like that circular motion you used to make with your finger in your hair when you became impatient. I will divide up time.

"Do you remember?" Bénédicte has laid her hand on my arm. I can tell that behind her eyelids even older scenes are flashing by — she is singing in the rowboat to tease Vincent, she's scaring off the fish, it's one of their little games of romance. She wants to be able to shout as the rowboat lands, "We didn't catch anything," but *we* won't be on the verandah any more, only our books will still be there. Martin, ardent lover that he is, will have taken me off to the bedroom.

Has Bénédicte been following the thread of my thoughts? She tells me she has met Martin recently when he was in Montreal for a symposium but he isn't quite the same. She gives details — his speech is more precise, his back a bit stooped, not because of tiredness but rather from a certain caution. He now has a careful, self-protective way of moving his head toward the person he is talking to. A sense of survival that he must have learned. Or distrust.

I don't ask questions. I don't want to know anything concrete about his life — is he happy, does he have a wife, where did he go for his holidays? Just picturing that carefulness, that self-control, those hunched shoulders touches off vague feelings of affection and pity in me. That, too, is life — the small, humble vision of it. Everything appears diminished, even boldness, even love, even the shadow of death falling toward us.

We now have brown spots on our hands. The thought enters my mind but I quickly push it away behind happier ones. The rowboat is only a few metres from shore, Étienne is trying to leave his childhood behind, Vincent's back is still very straight. The day has been immersed in music and, beneath Bénédicte's hand, warmth is spreading through my arm. There are spots on our hands but I pretend I don't know what lies ahead for us.

2
Chapter Two

As we take our first breath we put love in the centre of our soul, in a hollow space suddenly empty, in a wilderness. A great cry fills the air. A woman takes us in her arms, we will call her Mother, but she is no longer the soft, infinite mother. She is a body next to us, already an absence. And even though we know this, we search for a presence. We move from house to house, we roam, changing men, women, cities, countries. We shout out, "Land," then burst into tears — it was only a mirage. We go on, we keep searching. As long as we keep searching, we won't grow old.

Vincent is leaning over my face. With his finger, he circles my mouth. He tells me I don't have any wrinkles yet and I reply, it's because I still haven't found the answer. He says, "Well, don't find it then," and I start to laugh. There are advantages to being a child — we suffer but don't grow old. We don't have a life to manage, the kind of life we would otherwise be living, with boundaries, petty concerns, and yesterday's left-overs. We don't make choices.

But I'm cheating. I've noticed a wrinkle at the corner of my eyes, and when I squint, the crease becomes more pronounced. It isn't conspicuous yet but shows up on photos between my eyelid and temple. Something is changing. I have entered the time that metes out the days and the nights one by one. For the past few days I've been counting, as when I say to myself, soon I'll be forty, Philippe thirty-four, François thirty-one. And Noëlle turned thirty-eight today.

I didn't phone Mama as I usually do. What's the use of dwelling on that old heartache? Maybe she hasn't thought about it, she was supposed to go over to François's place, she must have brought him the curtains she made for him. François probably has taken her out to a restaurant. Since his return François knows how to say thank you. He must have learnt that while searching for Noëlle.

Yesterday he brought me a gorgeous plant for the living-room. We set it down by the window beside your armchair. The effect is amazing — the chair looks totally different, the furniture doesn't seem to have ever been used by you. He arrived just as I was leaving the house. I had to go over to Madame Girard's to pick up her mail, so we went there together. We lingered in the park near the pond. The ducklings have grown bigger. The mother ducks aren't watching them as closely any more but have started to lead a life of their own again, they are learning to be separated from their little ones. François put his arm around my shoulders and said, "I won't forget." Just these words. And I kept silent, as when we've escaped unharmed from a labyrinth. François wouldn't forget. The days would slip by, the months, the years. He was already moving away from me. One day we might be far apart, so far we might not be able to reach one another any more, each of us living in a

170   separate continuum of time. There would be a whole world between us perhaps, but this moment would spring up again, defiant and luminous, in loves still uncharted. We wouldn't have forgotten.

And almost tenderly I thought about you.

3
Chapter Three

I should have been on my guard. All at once the day
foundered. The sun was like a summer sun, Vincent's shadow
floated around in my cup and I was working at my desk.
Then a ringing broke the silence. I should have been on my
guard but automatically picked up the receiver.

At the other end a voice I'd never heard before asked me if
I was Emma Villeray, the sister of Noëlle. "Yes." She wanted to
meet me as soon as possible, could a close relative be there as
well, my husband, a brother, or a woman friend? I must again
have answered yes and I must have hung up because I found
myself with my hands free in front of words that sank into the
red notebook, that were suddenly illegible, indecipherable.

I got to my feet, seized with an uncontrollable urge to throw up — the coffee, the jam, the bread, my heart, my stomach, the past which lies in wait in some hidden corner, the past which attacks us, cuts us into shreds, leaves us for dead in some desolate forest. It all spurted out like a geyser onto the floor and I lay down in my vomit, my body as dry as a coffin. My teeth were chattering in my mouth. This is what I'd become, chattering jaws, a bag of disconnected bones that would go on knocking against each other till the last gasp. Death had set in. When Vincent came home, my limbs would be cold. The woman would arrive tonight to talk about Noëlle but I wouldn't be there to hear her any more. I had outwaited the waiting, I had waited so long the passage of time had become impossible to endure.

I closed my eyes, folded my hands over my stomach. My soul was leaving my body through the sockets of my eyes. I was the one who was slipping away this time. Noëlle wanted to come back but I wouldn't be there to welcome her any more. I was abandoning her, this time *I* was abandoning *her*. I let out a scream so loud it broke all my bonds with the earth, so loud that it rang out into eternity and my soul rose up high in the air, beyond the clouds, into the motionless sweep of the heavens.

I heard chanting. I opened my eyes. Two huge breasts were leaning over me. Someone was reciting a prayer, mopping my brow, weeping. A woman in mourning clothes lifted me up in her powerful arms and carried me into the bedroom. Then this enormous black form sat down in the cane chair by the bed to watch over me. She began to sing in a velvety voice, just for me, only for me. I recognized my neighbour. The bed was warm and soft — so cosy that I felt my dead body could sleep there until the end of time.

When I woke up, Vincent was in the room. My neighbour introduced herself, "Rosa." He thanked her, he was going to take care of me. Footsteps sounded on the stairs, then the door opened. I heard a tap running in the kitchen, a voice speaking into the telephone, I recognized the word "doctor." I needed to talk to Vincent. Eight o'clock tonight, that's what the woman had said, was I going to be able to receive her?

I stared at the ceiling, trying to find the crack I had just slid through. All I could see was a spotless, white, impenetrable surface. I turned my head toward the window but the blind was pulled down, the room was in darkness. It was neither night nor day, it was the beginning of a block of time that had split off. It was alive though, deathlike but alive.

Chapter Four

She walked into the room in a businesslike way. Her voice was neutral, so was her dress. Then her thin body slipped into the cane chair. I almost said no, not there, not in my neighbour Rosa's chair. I lowered my eyes, already I had difficulty putting up with her. I didn't apologize for receiving her in my bedroom — I hadn't asked her for anything, *she* had forced me to have her over. Vincent settled down beside me on the bed and she began, well-rehearsed phrases tailor-made for the occasion, which she reeled off while looking at us blankly.

I suddenly hoped she would disappear right then and there. But she droned on and finally got to the point where she should have started. It sounded like the script of a second-rate movie, a story I could never have dreamed up. Noëlle and her husband had been in an accident, they had died in a Los Angeles hospital. Noëlle knew she wasn't going to live and had confessed everything — her running away, her marriage, her new identity. Her three miscarriages and then the miracle, this child, a little four-year-old girl.

I understood perfectly. Noëlle was asking *me*, her sister, to look after her daughter, to raise her as though she were mine.

I didn't react, I just listened. Noëlle had directed her last words to me in a language that wasn't my own, I couldn't get past that detail. And I translated the woman's words into English so I might hear Noëlle's foreign voice.

Did I have any questions? I asked what language the child spoke. The woman gave me a funny look. She replied, "English, no doubt." I added, "Of course, English," without realizing that what I was saying was ridiculous. A numbing fatigue swept over me and the woman left the bedroom, following after Vincent. I heard voices as though they were coming through a thick fog, I didn't make any effort to listen to them. I wanted to sink into a sleep that would last as long as Noëlle's absence.

Then that singing again. In the cane chair Rosa was holding a piece of knitting in front of her gigantic breasts. Vincent had left me a note, he would try to be home early. I should get moving, go down to the kitchen, look at a patch of sky, have something to eat. I asked if I could see daylight and the bedroom filled with that peaceful kind of sunshine that bathes our world after a long illness when we try to get up, wobble over to the window, peer at the flowers that have shot up in the garden. Childlike, we'll say to ourselves, "It's lovely out," and that phrase once again contains hope, sips of sparkling water and the face that allows us to rejoin humanity. Vincent's regular features flashed through my mind, his straight nose, his truthful eyes, and I wanted to keep that face close to me forever.

There would be Vincent, and behind me all those things I would have cast off, the way one escapes from the night.

176   My neighbour supported me. I went down the stairs on shaky legs, sat down for a moment on the sofa. In the middle of the coffee table a little girl was riding a red tricycle, a dark-haired, smiling little girl with the carefree look of childhood. I leaned toward the photograph, picked it up with trembling hands and turned it over. There was writing in English on the back. "Emma, four years old."

It was Noëlle's hesitant handwriting. Time hadn't changed it.

Chapter Five

I don't know anything about myself any more. I touch my
shoulders, my stomach, my face, my eyelids. Do I still exist?
I do, but inside an unbroken solitude where light doesn't
penetrate. Sunshine doesn't reach me any more, neither does
daylight. I am examining the world under my bell jar. It has
shrunk all of a sudden, even the maple tree which is now
bending under the weight of its splashes of yellow leaves. It's
a hundred years old, I'm a hundred years old, an age when
one no longer knows anything.

On her red tricycle a little girl stretches out her hand to
point at something — we can't see what it is, perhaps the
camera or a child on the sidewalk or her mother. That is

178   Emma, Noëlle's daughter. She has my smile. Mama is going to say, "That little four-year-old face looks just like you."

I am four years old on my red tricycle. I am stretching out my hand toward Noëlle, she is babbling away in Papa's arms. "Watch the birdie," Mama calls out. I turn my eyes, I don't see anything.

Under a bell jar one hears everything at the same time — Mama's clear voice, Papa's instructions, Noëlle's baby talk when she was two, also her other language, her foreign language, the one she spoke as a mother, "Emma, look at me please." Everything in a single, never-ending hum.

I am waiting. I am biding my time until my voice slowly rises above the others. Then I'll fly into a terrible rage against Noëlle — she won't impose her child on me, she who abandoned us all. I'll tear the photograph into pieces and pick up my life where I left it.

Or I will say, Noëlle is still my sister, she has given me a child. And silence will descend, a silence as gentle as a winter's first snowfall. I stop, turn around to look at my footprints, then start singing Rosa's lament. I have come to a fork and I take the road that leads to a strange land. I am bringing a little girl along with me. This is love in its simplest form. This is what it means to share a first name. And be forty years old.

I'm not afraid. I'm regaining my strength slowly in the shadow of the life I've left behind. The snow scatters tiny stars under the late summer sun. They settle everywhere, on the leather armchair by the window, on François's plant, on Emma's red tricycle. They leave crystals on my eyelids and I am smiling. It's the same smile as on the photograph but it isn't the smile of a child. There is that wrinkle embedded between my eye and my temple, there is an answer which came when I no longer expected it, a whole new future, candles to light on birthday cakes.

And there is that unknown image of myself. The image of a mother, of which I can still only discern a dim, transparent shadow on the cold paper.

Chapter Six

Our childhood will surface in the tone of a voice. We never know quite when, but it's suddenly there in its awful confusion with its broken dolls and nursery rhymes — we can no longer ignore it. Mama very nearly gets out the old story book, takes on her theatrical voice, reads us that tale about a frog who changed into a prince, as Noëlle bends forward to gently stroke the illustration. Noëlle loved princes so much.

She is all we talk about. We huddle around Mama and each of us in turn says, "Do you remember?" We are living in a past that joins bodies and feelings together. In a shared warmth. But then we need to come back to reality. There is

180   the legal procedure, the ashes to be brought back home, Philippe reminds us, the bungalow. And little Emmanuelle. That is her real name.

Mama agrees with everything. Noëlle will rest next to her father, and if no one claims his remains, Juan will too. Mama has forgiven them. Not a single angry word, it's more a relief that she feels. Her child is coming back to her — she is dead but she is coming back to her. Order has been restored in Mama's world. On Sundays in summer we'll go and leave flowers by the grave. She will mourn her dead all at the same time, Papa, Noëlle, and why not Juan as well? Isn't he Noëlle's husband? Little Emma's father?

She glances toward the sideboard, looks at the photo she has stood up against a knick-knack — Noëlle and Juan hand in hand in front of their bungalow. And her face lights up. She turns to François for support, Noëlle must have been very brave, she gave up everything for love.

When she says this our bodies move apart, we take up our places in our own lives again. We go back to the fragmented flow of time of ordinary feelings, to unheroic days followed by more unheroic days, to children. Philippe shrugs his shoulders. Perhaps he sees Anne, Véronique and Pascal, and the little girl who will soon be born. He sees joys that can be measured, difficulties, but he would rather not tell Mama. François catches my eye. We have given up our grandiose pursuits but Mama doesn't know, what good would it do to disappoint her? I wink at him, why speak about this with Mama? She is happy today.

"Anne and I can look after Emmanuelle." I thank Philippe. No, I don't feel bound by Noëlle's last wishes. I'm anxious to put away my childhood in the big toy-box and enter into the mystery of another childhood, a separate, unknown one, outside of me. This is not how I explain things though. I say, "I'm going to adopt little Emma. Vincent and I are going to bring her up together." It's what we both want.

Mama is pleased. Also, she'll be right there, she'll help us, she'll be able to take part in Emma's upbringing, Emma will be our child, our little Noëlle. The sentence forms in my mouth all by itself, I snap out, "Vincent and I will manage on our own." But then my voice softens, we'll come to see her on Sundays like Anne and Philippe, sometimes we'll all have a meal in a restaurant.

We are going to make a real home for Emma, with pictures to cut out and a small rocking chair, stuffed toy animals and a tawny cat who will sleep at the foot of her little bed. At night I will read her a story, a story about tiny tots that don't always do as they're told.

7

Chapter Seven

We could say this is friendship, these inner eyes that take the place of words — one look and I can tell, Bénédicte is happy or worried. So I go to her, I'm here, I'm right here. We could just as well say this is love, but the kind that doesn't crowd us, the other kind, which is discreet, which doesn't smash anything.

Bénédicte took two or three puffs, then put her cigarette down in the ashtray where she will leave it until it goes out. She rarely smokes, only in moments of intense emotion when her distress is so great it requires certain gestures. She blurts out, "What an unbelievable story! How are you going to cope? When are you leaving?" without expecting answers. She talks the way she smokes. She is concerned, would *she* be able to be so forgiving?

So then I must try to explain. There is nothing for me to forgive. When Noëlle died, she took boundless passion with her to the grave, she left me life with its ordinary joys, she left me with a down-to-earth human kind of love. I let Vincent continue — he, too, is anxious to see a child grow up. Then he gives details, the police investigation, the red tape, the immigration procedure. A neighbour has taken in little Emmanelle, I will be leaving as soon as the authorities let me.

The cigarette has gone out. Bénédicte lights up another, something she never does. She repeats, "What an unbelievable story!" and I agree, but I don't think it is. Sooner or later Noëlle had to come back, take her place with us again. Mama had to find out before she died how the story ended.

The riddle has been solved. Once again I connect causes to their effects — thousands of invisible threads link my body to the landscape. Now I walk along with a certain confidence, as if I could touch reality. Reality is everywhere these days. In Mama's extravagant dreams, in the first name of a tiny girl, in your return which I am no longer waiting for. When Noëlle died, you died. I've destroyed my sentimental heart, torn up my old fairy tales, banished my weariness. I've remained on the warm, ochre earth. You have soared into a sky far too blue for my world.

Chapter Eight

The maple tree is still there, in front of the window.
Emmanuelle's photograph is still there. A golden voice rises
up from the speakers. Reality is holding out, it busily darts
about, it runs faster than I do. I'm out of breath but I've been
able to keep up. I'm making lists, reservations — I ask
Vincent what day it is.

It's Saturday. Judith is eating her croissant. It is really *her*,
your first wife, across from me. She licks her fingers, she says
she likes houses from that period, with wooden panelling.
She has stepped over the threshold of my place. When I
phoned her I wasn't sure she would accept. I tried to come
straight to the point, I had to get rid of your things, would

she be interested in dropping by? There was your desk, the swivel chair, the filing cabinet, I thought Étienne might want them. Without hesitating she said she would come over.

I pour her another cup of coffee. I go to get little Emma's photo. I explain that I will need a room for her, that's why I called. Reality pushes memories onto the doorstep, it shifts them into other houses where someone will gently pull them into another life.

We go upstairs. The key turns in the lock. The door creaks, it needs some oil. I throw open the window and street noises drown out the golden voice. Your things are covered with dust, they don't look the same any more. I empty out the boxes, point at things. Judith says yes or no. We fill up other boxes, the ones she'll take home with her and the ones I'm going to give to a charity. But don't I want to keep anything for myself, not even the books? I shake my head. Then I change my mind, I think I will, you had some beautiful books. Judith is right, time has gone by, why not hold on to them?

Even so, emotion slyly catches me in the pit of my stomach, from under a pile of journals or winter clothes. For a second this feeling surges out from a pen. Judith is holding it in her hand; it had been a present from her when you landed your first big contract. Then the wool jacket you would slip on on fall nights — this time *my* fingers are trembling. And I can't help thinking of memory as of a stream that bubbles even when it sleeps.

"Sometimes people leave because they can't bear the prospect of being left." The sentence hisses through Judith's lips and I let it go by without responding. I wouldn't know how to reply, that remark is about you and Judith, but also about you and me. I'm sure Judith sees things more clearly than I do after all these years. I'm sure she knew what would happen to the two of us. Hadn't there also been Dominique whom you'd left to marry *her*? What you used to call passion was perhaps nothing more after all than the continual excitement of change. My lips tighten. One isn't keen on dwelling on reality when it unravels beautiful stories, when it makes love as ordinary as a flat stretch of land.

186   But Vincent arrives with Étienne — and this is the sweet side of ordinariness — they've rented a small truck, together they are going to move your furniture to Judith's place. Étienne makes it quite plain to us that they don't need our help. "He doesn't give Vincent time to catch his breath," Judith comments. I want to reassure her. I reply that it's Vincent he seeks out when he comes over, much more than me. She knows, she isn't jealous. Not any more.

She lays her hand on the window sill, gazes out into space, then her voice becomes a bit muffled. "Perhaps we have children," she says, "so we can get used to being separated from those we love."

Chapter Nine

"Aren't you afraid?" No, I'm not. I don't squint at the sky any more, it's as if I were no longer in any danger of being blown away, as if roots were growing under my feet and striking deep into the earth, veining the soil.

Emmanuelle's room is ready now. There are funny animals on the walls, a child's bed with a headboard where she can put her books, a sketching table. Vincent and I spent a whole afternoon picking out furniture. We felt mattresses, inspected every drawer, compared materials. We are practising becoming parents.

Incredulously Anne repeats, "Aren't you afraid?" My sister-in-law tells me that she is afraid with each child. Not

188 about the delivery, no, it's a different kind of fear, the one
that torments us when we aren't sure we've taken the right
decision. But I've never decided to give birth to a child. I'm
welcoming her under my roof, that's easier actually.

I'm not afraid. Maybe because I just can't see myself as a
real mother. I'm still torn between two names. Sometimes
the little girl with the red tricycle has the English name
"Emma-four-years-old," she is pointing at Noëlle, *she* is the
mother. But then I set the photo down and I remember the
little girl is called Emmanuelle, "Emmanuelle Rodriguez," as
the thin woman explained. That is her real name and when
this sinks in she doesn't look quite so much like me any
more. I hear Noëlle's last will again. Once again I am the
mother of this child.

Everything will be clearer when Emmanuelle arrives,
Vincent thinks. She'll step out of her scene and the red
tricycle will go and join the other photographs in an album.
Yesterday he turned up with a small yellow bicycle. I said,
"She's still too small," but out of a bag he produced two tiny
training wheels which he'll attach so that she can keep her
balance in the beginning. He acts like a father — he wants
to protect her without keeping her under his wing. He is
going to show her how to cycle away but he'll be watching
her out of the corner of his eye from the balcony. "She will
learn the art of proper distance," he maintains with a laugh.
"She'll head back toward us and then she'll go off again." He
adds emphatically, "Don't worry, she'll come back."

Noëlle and I never had bicycles. Papa wasn't making
enough money and he wouldn't have had time to teach us
anyway. He was always working, during the day, at night,
sometimes on Saturday. We never learned the right way to go
off. I never left, Noëlle never returned. Philippe and François
did learn. Ever since they were teenagers they've been leaving
and coming back, I don't know who taught them.

I've travelled with you of course, to France, Switzerland,
to the United States, but that can't really be called going
away, living abroad. I could never have left Mama alone, I
never could have stood it. Fear was always there, white like

Noëlle's ghost, white like angels' dresses. It kept me
suspended between two clouds, it kept my mouth shut. Now
an echo carries my voice. I'm further away from Mama but
when I talk to her she can hear me perfectly — I tell her I'm
preparing for Emmanuelle's arrival in the same way as one
prepares for a departure. It will be a vibrant life filled with
puzzling changes, surprises, colds and sometimes tears,
homework after school, hugs and kisses.

All this I discuss with Mama, but not the small yellow
bicycle Vincent has bought. She wouldn't be able to sleep
any more. What I cannot tell her, I share with Anne — she
doesn't have the same fears as Mama. Together we are
discovering that our childhoods have very long roots which
reach straight down to the centre of the earth.

10

Chapter Ten

Vincent is caressing my nipple. He is tracing circles and I catch fire, first my breasts then my back, and from my back to my sex. My whole body has caught fire. I am completely willing. Love, desire — I still can't tell the difference between them except in books. There a clear line divides them, but my life isn't as neatly partitioned. And yet I do know this — with Vincent there is no need for me to struggle all the time, he won't run away. I don't sense terror in each one of his gestures as though he were in constant danger of being swallowed up by an abyss.

With Vincent it is love without the string that nearly snaps at every moment. He holds me close to him, calls

me his beautiful Emma, and I think of that tight lump as if
it were a sphere that had gone to join all those other
spheres lost in infinite space. My body is clear now, and
spacious and resonant, as resonant as a temple in which
one might hear the echoes of an oracle's harsh voice. I am
listening — there is no talk of either tragedy or war,
disappearance or departure.

We have the night. It comes toward us with its kindness,
it will spread my arms, spread my legs. Vincent will thrust
himself deep into my body and I will know him from all
other men. We will become one flesh, we will cry with a
single cry. Then our bodies will move away from one
another, we'll start talking again, we'll make more plans.
After that we will sleep. The angels will watch over us until
sunrise. We will wake up to a radiant day.

There aren't just heartaches. There isn't just
unhappiness. There is also the horizon opening up within
reach of our hands. When Vincent says, "In ten years," I now
completely believe him. I have entered the time of
resurrection. On my face, the tears have left only a bit of
salt. My cheeks are still round and fresh. "I feel like biting
into them," my lover says. He brings his teeth closer to my
cheek. I push him away, it's a little game we play.

Vincent caresses me, I caress Vincent, and the heart of
the world beats faster.

I'll be leaving soon. Then I'll return with Emmanuelle.
Vincent will have moved in here. I don't think any more,
"This is madness!" I look around me, at the maple on the
lawn, the light, and the invisible landscapes behind people's
windows. I say yes as if trying to hold on to the idea of
happiness, a kind of happiness that is small enough to fit
inside the four walls of a house. In this ordinary happiness I
also picture troubles, worries, but everything will stay on a
human scale. We won't become giants, we won't be afraid.

We aren't going to move. Yesterday we had the retired
workman over, the one who is so like Papa. In the basement
he is going to build an office for Vincent, and on the spot
where Monsieur Girard's blood spurted into the dust there

192   will be a playroom for Emmanuelle. His death won't be forgotten, it will be covered over by the footprints of a child. Madame Girard would agree. She would say, "Sooner or later it had to come to that." This may be what desire is when it mingles with love — a wave carrying us back up from the bottom of the sea, setting us down on the shore in a place where we can dry our faces and take the hand of a man or a child.

Vincent drew up a plan just as you used to do. The workman studied it, he looked exactly like Papa. And, strangely, I had a vision of Monsieur Girard's head in the dust. I thought of him and all those others who have sunk like a stone beneath the dark waves, never to return.

11

Chapter Eleven

Evening comes on a little faster now. It falls abruptly, settles in the throat, makes our voices sound solemn when we think of autumn drawing near. The maple tree will freeze in front of the window. Timidly Emmanuelle will gaze at that skeleton. She'll experience the cold for the first time, perhaps she'll think of Noëlle whom she's never going to see again. And I will be helpless in the face of so total an abandonment.

The woman stopped by again this afternoon, she is trying to speed up the procedure. Apparently Emmanuelle is retreating into a worrisome silence. They are waiting for me there as if I were the only person who could console her.

194   Just one word came into my mind, *orpheline*, "orphan" in
Emmanuelle's language. It had a silky ring to it. How can so
soft a word stand for such boundless grief? Language has no
ear for music, that is our downfall. But the woman wouldn't
have understood so I kept quiet. I simply told her that
everything was ready here, I could leave any time.

There's a hammering noise coming from down in the
basement. I hear wooden boards creak, then suddenly
Vincent's laugh — I would never have pictured him as being
as skillful as Papa. Other threads seem to be linking up with
one another. This evening I remembered that Papa was also
an orphan, and for the first time I saw Papa as a child. This is
how we see things when our world grows smaller.
Everything takes on different proportions, even unspeakable
grief. I cannot really fear for Emmanuelle, I still have too
many happy images of Papa. Papa tosses a ball to us on the
beach, Noëlle runs after it, catches the small red-white-and-
blue sphere. He is pleased, he has managed to tear his
daughter away from her novels.

It isn't that Papa disliked stories. On the contrary.
Sometimes when he was on holiday he would take over from
Mama, he'd gather us around him and make up wild tales
about tramps and thieves who were perfectly harmless. In *his*
narratives there were never any princes, fairies, or goblins.
Only poor people who wanted to have a house to sleep in and
bread so they wouldn't go hungry. We were too young, we
didn't understand that he was telling us about his own past
anxieties. He was happy. He now had a wife, children, and
tasty dishes steaming on the table. That's all he asked of life.

The dust has left salt-and-pepper highlights in Vincent's
hair, I watch him shaking it off on the balcony. He gives a
wave to the workman who is just leaving. It's a gesture I
simply can't associate with Elena, a gesture so far removed
from passion. But maybe a woman somewhere in Brazil is
puzzling over the same question tonight as she holds an old
photo of me in her hands.

"We are getting older," Bénédicte keeps saying, pointing
out the small creases in her hands to me. She turned up

yesterday with one of those miracle creams that fend off time. A great laugh rang out, a single laugh in two voices, Vincent and June. That is another thread linking the past to the present. There is something about June that reminds me of Vincent, her quiet self-assurance, the openness of those who have found the one person who can console them.

Vincent is shaking off the dust on the balcony while I'm lengthening my chain of similarities. I'm now adding on Papa, and Vincent and June, also François since his return. And for the last little while me too. No, I don't fear for Emmanuelle, she will fit right in with us.

12

Chapter Twelve

People don't die here. They may cough, they may be in pain or out of breath, but they don't die. The thud of the hammer is pounding this thought into my flesh. The workman makes the wood creak, he bangs in nails, he is building. A beautiful hardwood floor now covers over the last rings of blood. Yesterday the man said to me, "Somebody must have hurt himself here," pointing at tiny blood spatters embedded in the cement. Surprised, I knelt down in the dust. I believed I had got rid of the last stains. But death had slyly resurfaced.

The fight never ends. Each day one must repeat to a child, "People don't die here." I practise this with every blow of the hammer. That's what it means to become a mother, I think — being out of breath or in pain, feeling a tight lump in one's stomach sometimes, and yet cradling a child's cold fingers in the fleeting warmth of one's hand. I should put the question to Mama. Perhaps one day, over a cup of tea, I'll be bold enough to do this.

When she stopped by this afternoon she wanted to see Emmanuelle's room. She inspected everything, the bed, the curtains, the chest of drawers, then she took a quilt with a pink circle motif from her bag and with grandmotherly gestures placed it over the bed. As she did this, the years suddenly fell away. I thanked her in a voice charged with emotion, my dark-and-sturdy-little-girl voice and also *her* voice when she would say thank you to her own mother. It was as though I could feel in every fibre of my body what Madame Girard calls *memoria* — is that also what it means to become a mother?

I wrote her a long letter which I sent to Heracleion. I told her about everything, Noëlle, Emmanuelle, the renovations in the basement, Vincent's moving in, but she won't receive it. This morning the mailman brought me a postcard with a fresco on it, the most beautiful fresco from Knossos, the one with the bluebird. She has left Crete and is heading for the East, she wants to continue her wandering all the way to Babylon, where languages originated. When I arrive in Los Angeles she will be strolling among the ruins of Babel. Perhaps she will find the site of the Tower, that tower human beings endeavoured to build to reach heaven. Perhaps she will relive their punishment — the confusion of tongues, the scattering of the population.

I will have regained a small part of Noëlle. I'll try to piece together fragments of her life story. I'll throw open my arms to her daughter. For her I'll translate very simple words which have never been lost. Learning to share the language of a child after the defeat, after the final separation of heaven and earth, isn't that, too, what it means to become a mother?

"I won't be able to understand her," Mama frets. How is she, who has never ventured beyond her own language,

198 going to talk to Emmanuelle? So I reassure her, Emmanuelle will learn French in no time at all because deep within ourselves our mother's language is always preserved and, besides, for the first little while I'll translate. Mama smiles. She takes a sip of hot tea, runs her gnarled hand over the embroidered tablecloth. She isn't surprised today that I've laid it out for her. Very likely it is taking her back to all those winters when Grandmama would pull her needle through the fabric under the electric light. She looks at her hands, she says, "I'm just as old as my mother now." She confesses this to me with a sigh while the workman hammers away in the basement.

I should take her fingers into the warmth of my hand and say, "People don't die here," but being where she is she wouldn't believe me. Those would be the words of a mother, yet I'm only her daughter. She is walking on the edge of a bottomless abyss. And I know of no words that could ease her vertigo.

Chapter Thirteen

I'm enjoying the day, its gentle breeze. When I stepped out a little while ago, I shivered, then my body got used to it. Faceless in the crowd, I'm sauntering along. My life and I are in harmony.

The park is already in front of me, its multicoloured rustlings, the young ducks who are as big as their mother, the park which is now almost deserted. Schoolchildren sit facing blackboards, they daydream about their next holiday, about boats set loose on the pond, kites that don't get tangled in treetops.

Next year I, too, will take Emmanuelle to school. Then I'll come back, settle at my desk, resume work where I left off.

200 My book is coming out next month. "It's a fine translation," my publisher said. I think so too, I tried to get *below* the words to where the song lingers on. It will be my last literary translation. From now on I am only going to accept profitable contracts, non-fiction which requires less reflection about the language. I'll work on it in the afternoons or at night, after I've done my own writing. Next summer I'll bring my publisher a manuscript written by me.

Yet these past few weeks I haven't opened my red notebook. But I am writing without actually writing — I am going in the opposite direction, I play all the parts at the same time. Madame Girard and her husband, Mama and Papa. Also Noëlle. And you. I study old maps of Mesopotamia, I blow my brains out in the dust, run away, dream, die in a car crash. I am a body fleetingly visited by a succession of faces, I am nobody.

In a couple of weeks Noëlle will be resting in the cemetery with Papa, Emmanuelle will be riding her yellow bicycle under Vincent's watchful eye while I give them a little wave, pencil in hand, through the window. The film script will be coming along well, it will be finished by the end of the year. That much I know. What I also know is that I won't stop writing. Various stories, certainly Noëlle's — I want to enter the world of Ella Rodriguez, the woman with the false identity.

Now there is a place in my life for the kind of adventures I have given up. They will have wonderful titles and my name printed on them, while real life will be unfolding nearby, in the earthy smells of autumn, December's white frost, the first tulips in spring.

They're beginning to recognize me in Madame Girard's building. In the lobby I stop for a while to chat. Yes, Madame Girard is having a nice trip, when will she be back? She doesn't know yet, very likely when she has reached the beginning of human memory, the place where people believed in the creation of languages. Then I press the elevator button.

The plants are thirsty. Her son hasn't come by, he has

made himself scarce ever since he met me. He has buried his
mother along with his father, but that story doesn't belong
to me. He has probably found himself another mother,
leaving me *his* with her china ornaments. Perhaps he senses
that she and I are looking for the same thing, the amazing
moment when the first light of day succeeds in veiling the
sombre darkness of books.

There isn't a sound in the deserted apartment,
everything is waiting for a return that hasn't happened. It's
still too early, but Madame Girard will come back, I know it.
I know it just as I know that you won't come back. One day
she will be here again and I will call her by her first name.

Chapter Fourteen

I slipped the clasp into place the way one stitches up a wound, then set my suitcase down in the corridor near the entrance. Everything is tidy in the house. This morning I said to Vincent, "We have a beautiful place," the bedrooms, the living-room, the downstairs. The basement doesn't look like a tomb any more, there is a beautiful bright light streaming in, one feels like touching it.

I also told him, "I will miss you." But there was no fearfulness in that confession, I know Vincent will be here when I get back. And so I say words of love to him that don't ask for anything in return, simply to please him, the way one gives a bouquet of flowers, a glass of wine, or music one loves.

Tomorrow evening I'll be gone. What is waiting for me is immense. A bungalow of which I'll search every nook and cranny, clues that will allow me to assign a real face to Noëlle with some grey hairs already, a few crow's feet, marks left by the years when they teach us about time. But perhaps she will have continued to look at life from afar, through an old screen. In that case I am going to rediscover the little sister who will have dreamed her dreams until the very end. I still can't tell which one of these images I would rather find.

What is waiting for me is also quite small. A little girl who has only just taken her first steps and is facing the infinite loneliness of her foreign birth, a little stranger whom I'll approach awkwardly with the insecurity of a woman who has long ago forgotten her prayers.

Night is falling. Soon my neighbour Rosa's voice will rise up in the darkness. When she came to kiss me goodbye this afternoon she promised she would sing me a song of farewell. She brought a present for Emmanuelle, an illustrated story in Spanish which she will read to her herself so she won't forget her father. For a brief moment I saw a distant ache come into her eyes, like the shadow of a lost homeland, and I hugged her, hugged her very tightly. This is something I do more and more spontaneously now that I have lost my fight against eternity.

The slamming of the car door, Vincent's footsteps, the key grating in the lock. I get up, walk toward him. I am going to say to him, "I will return." For him, but also for myself. So I can hear what it sounds like when someone talks about coming back.

Chapter Fifteen

There are so many languages here they buzz like a swarm of insects. I strain to overhear what is being said at the next table, catch a few words, then release them right away. I let them drift off into space.

Big-bodied jets are poised on the runway. In a little while they will take off. We'll see them climb up in the deep-blue sky, then we won't see them any more. They'll be hiding out in the clouds, seeking cover from the wrath of God. Vincent points out my plane to me which stands motionless over there, there is still an hour to wait. I am ready to go now.

Last night I had another dream. Véronique and Pascal

were running up to me. A short distance away, Philippe supported Anne who came slowly walking toward me behind her large stomach, then François appeared with his blonde Fabienne, and Mama. Bénédicte, too, accompanied by June. And Judith with Étienne, also Madame Girard, and Vincent. They were all there. The scene was like the happy ending in a story.

Mama unwrapped a cake which she placed in front of me on the table. She stuck in the candles. Pascal shouted with glee, Étienne put his long, awkward arms around me, they kissed me. At tables close to us, people turned around and smiled, then they all began to sing "Happy Birthday, Emma," the family, friends, people at nearby tables and then the whole place in every possible language — it was the city of Babel accepting the scattering of the population. It had been Mama's idea to have a celebration for me in the midst of this joyful cacophony.

Vincent passes his hand in front of my eyes. What am I thinking about? I say, "In a few hours I'll turn forty. Just as the plane touches down in the city of angels."

Mama has never forgotten any of our birthdays, not even at the time of unspeakable grief, the year following Noëlle's disappearance. She phoned me this morning, she wanted to come and see me off. I declined. The world is too big here, she would have felt lost. We wouldn't have been able to form a perfectly round little island in this foreign space, she would have been disoriented. Before driving out to the airport I stopped by her house, as if to say, I may be leaving, but I'm here nevertheless, I'm thinking of you.

I'm thinking of you. This phrase will always convey the essence of love — love for one's mother or one's child and equally for a lover, remembrance, the surge of emotion released by remembrance when suddenly time stops on the image of a significant gesture. Knitting wool socks, whirling a woman around in arms as muscular as Papa's, tracing circles on a breast, welcoming a child into one's house. Saying to a man, I will return.

I reach for Vincent's hand. His blue eyes are staring into

206　the distance, toward the end of the runway. He is probably planning our next vacation. I watch him and murmur, "My love," just to myself, but he turns to me, he heard it, he smiles. Then an untranslatable silence muffles the chaotic hum of all the languages. The moment will last for a bit but not for long. Soon a female voice will announce my flight. Calm and trembling, I will get up, pick up my bag and head for the dimly lit corridor.

In my mind I have rehearsed this scene a hundred times. I get out my passport and my boarding pass, I snuggle up in Vincent's arms and stay there for a while. Then I gently pull away from him. I start walking, alone. I blow him a last kiss.

And I go through the gate.

Liedewy Hawke holds degrees in French language and literature and a graduate diploma in translation. She won the John Glassco Award and the Canada Council Translation Prize (now the Governor General's Literary Award for Translation) for *Hopes and Dreams: The Diary of Henriette Dessaulles, 1874-1881.*